Society WEDDINGS

A Corrigan & Co. novella

By Crystal Perkins

Copyright © 2015 by CRYSTAL PERKINS

Cover Design by Helen Williams
www.allbookedout.com

Interior Layout by Jesse Gordon
adarnedgoodbook.com

All trademarks are owned by their respective companies and are denoted by the use of proper capitalization of the company and/or brand. All rights reserved. Without limiting the rights under copyright reserved above, no part of this publication may be reproduced, stored in or introduced into a retrieval system, or transmitted, in any form, or by any means (electronic, mechanical, photocopying, recording, or otherwise) without the prior written permission of both the copyright owner and the above publisher of this book. This contemporary erotic romance is a work of fiction. Names, characters, places, brands, media, and incidents are either the product of the author's imagination or are used fictitiously. The author acknowledges the trademarked status and trademark owners of various products referenced in this work of fiction, which have been used without permission. The publication/use of these trademarks is not authorized, associated with, or sponsored by the trademark owners. This ebook is licensed for your personal use only. This ebook may not be re-sold or given away to other people. If you would like to share this book with another person, please purchase an additional copy for each person you share it with, especially if you enjoy sexy, emotional, romance novels with alpha males. If you are reading this book and did not purchase it, or it was not purchased for your use only, then you should return it and purchase your own copy. Thank you for respecting the author's work.

ABOUT SOCIETY *WEDDINGS*

Behind every great spy is the sexy man who loves her...

The women of the Society invite you to join them as they finally walk down the aisle. Whether it's the first or second time they're saying "I Do" to the man they love, these weddings are the ones they've always dreamed of.

Planning a mission and planning a wedding are two different things...

You've shared their struggles, triumphs, and SECRETS, and now it's time to share the celebrations of their love. Mishaps, murders, misunderstandings, and general mayhem will ensue before they get their happily ever after, but that will make them even more special.

Ten female spies + ten equally strong men = ten weddings full of romance, weapons, tears, and lots of sexy times. RSVP at your own risk.

OTHER BOOKS BY CRYSTAL PERKINS

The Griffin Brothers series
Gaming For Love (The Griffin Brothers #1)
Building Our Love (The Griffin Brothers #2)
Creating A Love (The Griffin Brothers #3)
Learning To Love (The Griffin Brothers #4)
Designing The Love (The Griffin Brothers #5)
Working On Love (The Griffin Brothers #6)
Keeping Their Love (The Griffin Brothers #7)

Corrigan & Co. series
Fielding Her SECRET (Corrigan & Co., #1)
Devouring the SECRET (Corrigan & Co., #2)
Rocking a SECRET (Corrigan & Co., #3)
Lessons in SECRET (Corrigan & Co., #4)
Uncovering His SECRET (Corrigan & Co., #5)
Training the SECRET (Corrigan & Co., #6)
Inheriting a SECRET (Corrigan & Co., #7)
Tending Their SECRET (Corrigan & Co., #8)
Playing in SECRET (Corrigan & Co., #9)
Loving My SECRET (Corrigan & Co., #10)

Other books
Never Fear-Phobias Horror Anthology
(Chronophobia short story)
Never Fear-Christmas Terrors Anthology
(Silent Fright short story)

For everyone who took the journey with these ten women along with me. Thanks for loving them!

AINSLEY & ZACK

<u>Ainsley</u>

"Stop fidgeting, or I'm going to end up stabbing you with these damn pins," Stella tells me, as she works on altering my wedding dress.

Most brides would just have it done by the bridal shop, or the designer. I'm not most brides, though. I'm a member of the Society, a secret group of women who right as many of the wrongs in the world as we can. And my good friend, Stella, is our stylist. She's also a perfectionist, hence the alterations she's doing on my dress right now.

"I still don't know how I let you talk me into a pink wedding gown."

"Just because you're a tomboy, doesn't mean you should be wearing blue."

"I normally lean towards purple, and not blue, and you know it."

"Purple is a little out there for a wedding gown, even for me. The blush pink looks beautiful on you, especially with all of the swirling fabric on the bottom."

There is a lot of fabric curling around to make what looks like giant roses—or frosting—on the bottom. Actually, frosting is probably a better metaphor since I feel like a cupcake in this dress. Not that it's a bad thing. My fiancé, Zack Taylor, loves sweets, and looking like a cupcake might get me a few extra licks in the honeymoon suite. That isn't me complaining—I'm well taken care of when he's not off on a road trip with his football team—but a little extra time with Zack and his tongue is not something I'd turn down.

"Is the dress too much?" I have to ask.

"Too much what? Money? No. You can afford it. Too much fabric? On someone else, maybe. But you look so beautiful, Ainsley. I wouldn't tell you that if it wasn't true. Zack is going to fall to his knees when he sees you walking towards him."

"If I ever find a place for us to get married," I mumble.

"You will. I can't believe he wouldn't get married on the football field. I thought that was a perfect idea."

"Me too. He says it's too clichéd."

Society Weddings * 11

"It is, but who cares? You both love the game. You wouldn't have met if it wasn't for football. Can't you change his mind?"

"If I really pushed it, he'd do whatever I wanted. I don't want this to be just my wedding, though. It should be about both of us, and what makes us happy."

"Is he not happy with football anymore?"

"What? No. That's not it. He loves football more than anything except for his family and me. I think it's more that, during the season, he spends more time on that field than he spends with me, and he wants this to be just for us."

"Football is the main thing you have in common, so what else would be "just for you"?"

"I don't know," I admit.

That's the problem. Zack and I are perfect for each other. We fit together. But I'm sure no one on the outside sees it that way. When you strip away football, you have a sexy god, and a sexy nerd. We're both sexy—it took me some time to believe that, but we are—but I know our relationship is still a shock to many people. While our sex life is spectacular, what we have is so much more.

We have lazy Tuesdays, spending most of his day off cuddling on the couch, while we marathon some of the TV shows we missed the week before. We have late night dinners after the games. Win or lose, we eat alone, just the two of us, once he comes home. We have the secret signal he gives me before each game, and the kiss I give to his helmet every week. Either in the tunnel here in Vegas, or before he leaves for his away games. I go to as many away games as I can, but I have an important job. A job he appreciates as much as I do.

When I met my man, I thought he was just a shallow manwhore. Over time, I came to realize that he just put up that front to protect himself. Don't get me wrong, he slept with plenty of women, and let plenty more get on their knees for him. But I'm the only one who got to see the real him. *Gets* to see it still. Once we got past all of the jealousy, and childish behavior, we exposed our real selves to each other, and only then did I truly know how lucky I am.

He's as cocky as ever in public, but in private, he's self-deprecating and sweet. He would lay his life down for his family, his close friends, and yeah, me. When my friends have gotten in some dangerous or sticky situations, he was right there, offering to do whatever he could to help. From the moment he put this football shaped ring on my finger, he has never wavered in his devotion to me. Sure, we still fight sometimes—we're only human. But I never worry that he'll walk away because I'm insecure, or because he'll find someone else. He's mine forever, and that's why this wedding has to be perfect. For both of us.

* * *

Society weddings • 13

Zack

It's the first weekend of the off-season, and I couldn't be happier. Well, I guess I could—we didn't win the Super Bowl, or even make it there—but now I get to spend more time with my wife-to-be. I have some endorsement photo shoots and commercials, and I'll train a little every day, but other than that, it's just me and Ains. She's still got work, and I know she's stressed about our wedding in two weeks, but every spare moment she has belongs to me. Hell, I may just go hang out in her lair at the Foundation when she's working, just so I can have those moments, too. The house is too empty without her here.

The doorbell rings, and I jump up to answer it. No one buzzed at the gate, so it has to be family or a friend. I open the door to see Stella on the other side, and if looks could kill, I'd be dead at the moment. It takes me a moment to realize that Reina's with her, too, because I'm still trying to resist the urge to cover my dick with my hands. If I've learned one thing from the Society women, it's that you don't show fear. Like ever. You embrace your fear, and then put on a brave front.

"Hi ladies, what's up?"

"What's up? Seriously, Football?" Stella asks, stepping towards me. I'm so damn proud of myself for not stepping back.

"Calm down, Stell. We came here to talk to him, not hurt him," Reina says, putting a hand on her arm.

"Fine. Talk first, but if he continues to fuck-up, can I hurt him?"

"Just a little. Ainsley loves him."

"Um, while I'm totally loving this conversation—not— what that hell is going on?"

"You're breaking Ainsley's heart," Stella tells me, walking into the living room, and sitting on one of the couches.

"What? How?" We went two rounds before she left for work this morning, and she was definitely happy when she left. Or at least I thought she was.

"Sit down, Zack," Reina says with a sigh. I sit, and she continues. "I had a wedding in a casino. It was beautiful, and exactly what most people would've dreamed of. It wasn't what I wanted, I never even thought about what I wanted."

"I'm really sorry for that, Reina, but what does that have to do with me and Ains? She picked the casino for our wedding."

"Because you won't let her have a football wedding."

"She doesn't really want that." Does she?

"Of course she wants that. Ainsley isn't about flowers and bling. She wants to get married on the football field you fell in love on, and have that parking lot food thing," Stella says.

"Tailgating?" I ask with a smile.

"Yeah, that."

"I thought she just wanted that for me."

"And she thinks you don't want it at all. She's doing the casino for you," Reina tells me.

"Well, fuck. I just wanted her to have the fairytale."

"Which fairytale is that, Zack? Because while Ainsley is drop dead gorgeous, she'll never be a princess in a castle," Stella reminds me.

Shit. I shouldn't need to be reminded of that. "No, she won't. I've been trying to fit her into a mold, haven't I?"

"In life, no. We all see how much you love her just the way she is. She's never been happier," Reina tells me. "As far as the wedding, well, yes. You were trying to give her a dream wedding that's not her dream."

"She also thinks you'd hate to get married on the field," Stella says.

I shake my head. "I wouldn't. I only said that to let her off the hook. Which apparently, she was never on. She really wants this?"

"Yes, you idiot," Stella tells me.

I nod. I *am* an idiot. I should've known that Ainsley didn't want a banquet room, or a fancy dinner. My girl's happiest when she's eating stadium food in her jeans and my jersey. I mean, she can rock a gown like nobody's business, but she prefers casual. Now I just need to give it to her.

"Can we do this?"

"We're the Society," Reina says with a smirk.

That's all she really needs to say. "I have something I'd like to do. I didn't think it would work well in a ballroom, but on the field, yeah."

"I'll take care of the stadium, and all that's needed. Faith and Gavin will make sure the food is insane. The cake will come from Drago Sisters, like planned," Stella tells me.

"And the guests?"

"Not a problem."

"Thanks. For coming here and looking out for Ains."

"We did this for you, too, Zack. You have a wonderful family, but you're also part of our chosen one. Don't forget that," Reina reminds me.

"I won't."

I walk them out, and then pull up the number I need on my phone. He answers on the second ring. "Hey, Scott. I need your help. Again."

* * *

<u>Ainsley</u>

"Where are we going?" I ask, panicking a little. It's my wedding day, but we're not heading in the right direction. The casino is the other way.

"Plans have changed," Sierra tells me with a smile. She's Zack's sister and one of my ten bridesmaids.

"What do you mean? How could things have changed?"

"I think it's time to give her the letter," Isa says to my mom.

She nods, and then hands me an envelope. It has my name on it in Zack's handwriting. I look around to see all of my friends smiling at me. Jade hands me some tissues, and I know that if she's offering them, I'm definitely going to need them. I open the envelope, and pull out the page inside.

Hi Ains,

I'm not a formal guy, so this isn't going to be a formal letter, and we're not going to have a formal wedding. I'm sorry I made you think that's what I wanted. It's not. I was just being stupid, and forgot that you're not some fairytale princess who would want something fancy for us. I pretended that I didn't absolutely love the idea of marrying you on the field. Now that I've pulled my head out of my ass, I realize you really do want that, too. So that's what we're doing, baby. I'll see you in the End Zone as we begin the rest of our lives together.

I love you,
Zack

"We're going to the stadium?" I ask, smiling so wide I think I think my lips might crack.

"We are indeed," Tegan tells me.

I look over at my mom, who did so much work for my casino wedding. "You're okay with this?"

"I'm more than okay with this. I've always known that you wouldn't want the princess treatment. I had fun planning everything with you, but I was also worried. Today should be perfect for you. *This* is going to be perfect for you, and I had a big hand in it as well."

"Thank you. All of you."

And yeah, I'm using those damn tissues now. It only gets worse when we pull up to the stadium, and I see the parking lot turned into a giant tailgate party. It's like nothing I've ever seen, or could imagine.

There's a sea of trucks with their tires removed. All of them are painted purple, and round banquet tables are sitting in their beds. As I walk around, I see the centerpieces are like mini works of art. There are both candid and casual pictures of us, taken by Candi Griffin. Mixed in are computer parts, and roses made out of pigskin, complete with laces, all flowing out of overturned helmets in custom holders so they don't roll.

Food stations are being set up all over, and I can already tell that Faith and Gavin have outdone themselves. Trust the two of them to give me all of my favorite junk foods with just enough of a twist to please everyone else. There are vegan options, but not a salad in sight. I can't wait to try all of it.

"Come on, you can drool over the food later. Stella will kill us if we don't get you inside," Ellie tells me, pulling on my arm.

I follow her into the building, and up to one of the Skyboxes. The curtains are drawn, and the inside looks like a beauty salon. Stella waves everyone but me over to one side of the room, and then pulls me into a big hug.

"Surprise."

"You did this."

"Me and Rei might have paid a visit to the groom."

"He really wants this? You didn't make him say it?"

"No. I was ready to use some force, but it wasn't necessary."

"She's not kidding," Reina says, coming up behind me to hug me as well.

"Thanks. I mean it."

"You're welcome. Now let's get you ready."

* * *

Zack

I'm standing on the field, waiting for Ains. There's no countdown clock, and this is definitely not a baseball diamond, but I still feel like Drew Barrymore in *Never Been Kissed*. Despite knowing it's irrational, I can't help worrying that she won't come out onto the field. I may be cocky to everyone else, but I know I'm the lucky one in this relationship. I also know I messed up when we were first getting together. A. Lot.

"Knock it off, Zack," my dad says from where he's standing next to me as my best man.

"What?"

"Stop psyching yourself out. Ainsley is here, and she's going to be walking out onto this field in just a few minutes. That's going to happen."

"You're sure."

"1000%. That girl loves you."

"I love her, too."

"I know. She's perfect for you."

She is. Before I can agree with him, the music starts. My sister Sierra comes out of the tunnel first, followed by the Society women. They're all in short, strapless dresses made of different colored swirls of purple fabric. Instead or flowers, they're holding bouquets of "football roses" which are pieces of pigskin shaped to look like roses. When Stella showed them to me, I was mad that I hadn't bought any for Ains before. She convinced me that the wedding was the perfect place to present them to her, so I calmed down.

I'm not at all calm once the Wedding March begins, and Ainsley and her dad appear at the mouth of the tunnel. She's in a cool pink dress. Yeah, I said pink. Never fucking expected that, but damn does it look perfect on her. She's carrying the deep purple Calla Lilies I picked for her, and I can barely breathe. She's here. She's mine, and she's here.

Society Weddings ∗ 21

I see the excitement and joy on her face when the surprise Scott helped me with materializes in front of us. There are all of the living actors from the Star Wars movies, good and bad, male and female, old and new. They're in costume, holding light sabers over the aisle for her. She covers her mouth, and I see her crying. I paid all of my endorsement money for the year to get them here, but it's totally worth it.

I barely register her dad placing her hand in mine as I feel tears prickling in my eyes. "You look gorgeous."

"So do you. Thank you for this. All of this."

I shake my head. "This is for *us*. Both of us."

"The Star Wars was for you?"

"Okay. Most of it is for both of us," I tell her with a laugh, which she returns.

We face my coach, who got ordained just so he could do this for me. Our wedding may not be traditional, but our vows are. We make our promises, and then I kiss her, soft and sweet. "I love you, Mrs. Taylor."

"I love you, Mr. Taylor."

We take all of the pictures we need to, and then I lead her to the locker room for her next surprise. I had custom jerseys made for us to wear, along with jeans. Our wedding party will be wearing them, too, because I want us all to be comfortable at the reception.

"Oh my God, they're perfect."

"Yeah?"

"Yeah."

"I also had Stella get us a huge plate, so we can share without getting seconds."

"Everything is perfect, Zack. Really perfect."

"It is when we're together."

"Good thing we'll be together forever, then, isn't it?"

"Yes. It really is."

FAITH & GAVIN

Gavin

"You look like you're going to throw up," my friend Jake Mason tells me, as I look at the text on my phone.

"What? Oh, um, no. Just wedding stuff."

"It can't be that bad, man," one of my other friends, Caleb Hall says. "Faith is a cool chick."

"She is. It's just not easy to mix her grandparent's customs with the modern wedding she wants."

"Does she want a traditional wedding?" Jake asks.

"Yes, and no," I tell him honestly.

We're hanging out, drinking beers, and catching up while our women are out planning weddings. Well, Tegan's not planning a wedding since she's already married to Caleb, but she's there for support. The women of the Society have more connections and resources than anyone on this planet, but planning eight weddings, all within a few months is still a lot for them to pull together. Especially since they can't just abandon their regular work to focus on everything else. All of the guys have offered to help, but for the most part, they've told us they've got it taken care of. My number just got called, though, and I need to step up, and step in.

"I need to call Faith's grandfather. Can you guys excuse me for a few?"

"Go on. And good luck," Caleb tells me.

I'm afraid that I'm going to need that luck, and more. Faith's grandparents love me, but they also love the idea of a completely traditional Chinese wedding and reception. Faith wants some tradition, but she wants to do it her way. My brave warrior woman is afraid to disappoint the people she loves more than anyone but me, so she just told me she's going along with them. I've never been one to shy away from a conflict, and I won't start now. I press the name in my contacts, and hold takes some deep breaths.

"Hello sir," I say when he answers the phone.

"Gavin, we just got off the phone with Faith. It's wonderful to hear that you are happy to go along with our plans for the wedding and reception."

"We're not, sir. I'm sorry to be so blunt, but Faith's happiness is more important to me than anything. Having a completely traditional wedding will not make her happy."

He sighs before answering. "We know."

Excuse me? I hold my temper in check, and keep my voice calm. Years of training as a Senator's son has prepared me for almost anything. "You do?"

"Yes, Gavin."

"Then why have you been pushing her?"

"We keep hoping she'll push back. Before we…went away…she would stand up to us if she didn't agree with what we said or did. Now, she just goes along with us. I know she feels guilt, but that is not hers to carry."

No, it is not. The guilt belongs to her stepfather, and a sadistic bitch. Both of whom are no longer breathing. Her mother holds some well-deserved guilt as well, but she's truly sorry, and they're working on their relationship. Her maternal grandmother is still alive, but if we never see her in person again, it will be too soon for Faith. Yeah, her family's fucked up, but so is mine. My mother killed my father, and then went after Faith. The Society and I bought her off so she'd leave Faith alone, and while I could care less about the money, I would put a bullet in her head myself if she ever messed with my woman again. No question.

"She's not going to give you even an inch of pushback."

"We could tell her we hate you, and want her to break up with you," he says, and I can hear the smile in his voice.

"Let's not. I'm not 100% sure that she'd choose to fight for me again."

"Don't sell yourself short. Faith's love for you is strong and true. Just like yours for her is."

"I *do* love her, and we need to do something. We have to give her the wedding she wants."

"We will fly out to Las Vegas tomorrow and talk to her."

"Thank you," I say, sighing in relief. "There's something I'd like to do for Faith, and I need your help."

"Anything you need, Gavin. I'll see you soon."

* * *

Faith

"Stop telling me everything will work out. Gav," I yell out in frustration. "It won't. Not with this."

"If you're not happy with having a traditional wedding and reception, why don't you speak up?"

"You know why."

"You are not responsible for what happened to your grandparents."

I am, though. If I had just kept my mouth shut, those bastards wouldn't have gone after them. I thank God every day for the Society saving them, but it doesn't change the facts. If I had just taken my punishment quietly, saving them wouldn't have been necessary.

"Don't. Just don't."

"Don't what? Try to talk some fucking sense into you? Don't love you? What exactly is it that you don't want? Me? Us?"

Is that what he thinks? I can't let him think that. I reach out and run my fingers over his cheek. "I know I've been crazier than usual lately, but don't give up on me. Please, don't give up on me."

"I'll never give up on you," he tells me softly. "But I can only be your whipping boy for so long before there's nothing left of me."

My eyes fill with tears as he gets up and walks to his dresser. I don't move as he pulls out a t-shirt and basketball shorts. "Where are you going?"

"I need to clear my head. I'm going to the school for a little bit. I have some recipes I should work on before the next session starts."

Gavin opened a free cooking school for low income students after everything happened with his mom. It's been open for almost two years, and he's had to hire eight other chefs to keep up with the demand of students who want to learn. He always oversees the menus for each session, so I know he's telling the truth about having work to do. But I also know he's going there to avoid me. I deserve it after the way I've been acting, but it still hurts.

"I could help," I say, my voice wobbling a little.

He hears that wobble, and immediately turns around. "I love you, Faith. Never doubt that. I just need a little time alone to get my head sorted out."

"Okay." It's not, but I'm responsible for what's happening, so I can't really argue. "I love you, too."

"I wouldn't still be here if I didn't know that. I'll be back in a few hours. Try and get some rest."

He walks over and wipes away the tears falling from my eyes as he kisses me. I hold onto his wrists for a moment, not wanting to let him go. I know he'll come back, but I still hate that he has to leave. I need to get my head together, and remember that it's the marriage and not the wedding that's important.

I force myself to get up and take a shower after Gavin leaves. I can't eat breakfast, though. Just the thought of food makes me ill. That alone tells me I'm making the wrong choices. I only stop eating—and cooking—when my life is in extreme turmoil. Times like now.

There's a knock at my door, and I brace myself for another lecture from one of my friends. They all agree with Gavin, telling me I should stand up to my grandparents and have the wedding of my dreams. They don't understand, and I'm tired of trying to explain myself.

When I open the door, it's not my friends on the other side. "Grandfather? Grandmother? What are you doing here?"

"We had no choice but to come here," my grandfather says, squeezing my arm as they walk past me into the living room.

"Why? I'm doing everything you ask of me?"

"And that is the problem," my grandmother says. "Where is the strong girl who stands up to us when she knows we are wrong?"

"You're not wrong."

"Yes, we are. You don't want a fully traditional wedding, and we don't really want that for you either," my grandfather tells me.

"What?"

"We wanted you to finally stand up to us again. You are not to blame for what happened, Faith, and we were hoping if we pushed you on this, you'd finally be yourself with us again," my grandmother explains.

"But instead, you are pushing Gavin away because you are so unhappy."

I turn to my grandfather. "You've talked to Gavin? Did he make you come here and say these things?" If he did, we are going to have a problem. A *big* problem.

"You really think I would threaten your grandparents in any way?" Gavin asks, standing in the doorway, looking angrier than I've ever seen him look before.

I'm too far gone in my guilt and pity party to recognize that I'm still pushing *him* too far, so I just keep going. "There's no other explanation as to why they'd come here and say these things to me."

"If you truly believe that, then there's no reason for us to get married."

No. Oh my God, no. "You don't mean that."

"Yeah, Faith I do. I can't marry a woman who would rather accuse me of wanting to hurt the people she loves than face the truth. You are punishing yourself for things that aren't your fault, and until you accept that you're human and can't control everything in everyone's life, we don't have a future."

"I don't like ultimatums."

"And I don't like being marginalized by the woman I love. Again."

Have I done that? Yeah, I have. "I'm sorry."

"So am I."

"Please don't leave me. We can put off the wedding if you want, but please don't break up with me."

I know it's not PC or very liberated of me, but right now I don't care. I may be a mess about everything else, but I know that I'm a strong, kick-ass woman. And I also know that I need Gavin. Not to fill some part of my life that society thinks he should, but because I love him. I don't need a man to define me, but I need the one who completes me.

"I don't want to put off the wedding. Hell, I'd run to the nearest chapel and have Elvis marry us right now. But I can't fight the ghosts who are holding you hostage. I'm just a man. A mere mortal."

"You're everything to me. I'll run with you to that chapel if you need me to prove it to you."

"You'd do that? What about your grandparents?"

I turn to look at them, seeing that they look as scared as I feel. I know they love Gavin. "I'm going to marry Gavin today. We can try to find a Chinese looking chapel."

They nod, and then I'm pulled into a strong set of arms. "I don't need to get married today. I just need you to be happy on our wedding day. Happier than you've ever been before."

I tell him the truth. "Every day with you makes me happier than I've ever been before."

* * *

Gavin

Saying that the last few weeks have been crazy would be an understatement. Once Faith admitted that she deserved her dream wedding, it was full steam ahead. With all of her friends rallying around her, Faith has pulled it off. And so have I. I have some surprises for her, and I can't wait for her to see them.

I stop in the kitchen at Cyndi's Vegas home, which she offered us for the wedding. She still lives in Chicago, but she bought this place when Corrigan & Co. moved its headquarters here. It's got a lush, beautiful garden, despite being in the middle of the desert, and Stella has turned it into Faith's dream. I looked out the back windows when I walked in, and saw Chinese lanterns and modern centerpieces. Once I check on the food, I'll take a closer look at everything else.

"Is everything going okay?" I ask Levi. He was one of the first teens to graduate from my cooking program, and now he works for us part-time while he attends college.

"Yeah, man. It's pretty much perfect. We all know how important the food is for you and Faith. We've got this."

"I know you do. Thank you."

"Nothing to thank me for. You know how much you've helped me with your program. This is the least I can do," he tells me with a smile. "Your ingredients are all ready for you."

"Thanks."

I greet the other guys and girls working in the kitchen. It really does mean a lot to me to have my students and former students prepare the appetizers and meal Faith and I created for tonight. Her grandfather should be here soon to help me with what I want to create. It's a special meal for the two of us, one that will mean more than just something good to eat.

"Sorry I'm late, Gavin. Traffic was horrible," Faith's grandfather says, rushing into the room.

"It's fine. I have everything prepped. We just need to put it together, and then I can go and get changed. Wouldn't want to keep Faith waiting at the altar."

"No. We definitely don't want that."

We work together, with him showing me how to do the things I'm not sure of, and me doing the same with him. When it's done, we both take a few bites, and decide that everything is, in fact, perfect.

"Thank you for helping me with this."

"Of course. This dinner is something very special for both you and Faith. She will be very touched that you thought of this."

I hope so. I don't have time to dwell on whether she will or not as I hurry through getting ready. I change into my suit, and dress shoes, before heading out to take my place under the elaborate arch that's been erected. As I turn towards the assembling crowd, I see that Faith has had photos of our fathers placed on chairs in the front row. I also notice her mother is already seated, and we smile at each other. Faith's grandparents will be walking her down the aisle to me, and as I hear the music for the bridesmaids starting, I turn to the men next to me and smirk, knowing they're all anxious to see their ladies.

There is no best man and no maid of honor. Our friends are equally important to us, and we weren't going to try and pick one to have a special place of honor. Faith's girls have been with her for years, and their guys have become my best friends. It's an honor for us that they want to share the special night with us, and as I see Alex start down the aisle in a white dress, I wonder what else Faith has in store for tonight. I can't wait to find out.

* * *

<u>Faith</u>

In a traditional Chinese wedding, the bride will change at least twice. She starts with a red dress, changes to an "Western" white dress, and then wears a ball gown. Because I'm me—more modern than traditional—I flipped this part of the tradition on its head. I'm wearing a deep maroon dress that is almost purple for the wedding. It's sleeveless lace from my collarbone to my thighs, with sheer organza falling from there to trail behind me on the floor. My bridesmaids are the ones in white. Sleeveless organza dresses with some swirling pattern on them. Their dresses start at the neck, and after a fitted top half with an overlay, they flare out a little. Not exactly to a princess silhouette, but not mirroring my own, either. After the ceremony, I'll change into a fire engine red gown. It's also sleeveless, with a mix of shiny fabric with a subtler satin pattern, ending in layers of tulle from thigh to floor. I'm still covering all the bases, just not in the expected way. Totally me.

Stella hands me my bouquet, which is white lilies with some green and red flowers behind it. I don't ask her what kind of flowers they are, because that isn't important to me. The flowers are beautiful, and perfect, and I thank her for them, and for everything she did to help me pull this together. My bridesmaids line up, holding the fans they're carrying instead of flowers, and as I watch them go, I feel myself tear up.

My grandmother hands me a tissue. "I hope those are happy tears."

"You know they are."

"He is a good man."

"The best."

She nods, and then my music starts. Instead of the traditional wedding march, I'm going with a Chinese C-Pop wedding song. Kace helped me arrange for the singer to be here and perform it for us. My grandparents take their places beside me, and we begin to walk. My steps falter when I see Gavin. He's wearing a Mandarin coat, with a patterned vest underneath. From old wedding pictures, I know he is dressed exactly how my father was when he married my mother. As I walk closer, I realize that the vest is *exactly* the same design as my father wore. I have to bite my lip to keep from openly sobbing at this beautiful gesture from him. He smiles so brightly at me that my feet automatically start moving again.

Gavin holds out his hand for mine as we reach him, and after they both kiss my cheeks, my grandparents take my right hand and place it in his. "Thank you for the most beautiful gift of your granddaughter," he tells them. The feminist in me wants to yell at him for saying that, but the romantic woman who is in love with him overpowers her to swoon a little.

"You're wearing…"

"Is it okay? Stella was able to find the vest at a vintage shop."

"It's perfect. Thank you."

"*You're* perfect. You look amazingly gorgeous."

"Thank you."

"We should probably get married now," he tells me with a smile.

"Yeah. Let's do that."

The ceremony is a traditional Western one, but I have something planned at the end. Before we walk down the aisle, I turn to Gavin, speaking loud enough for those gathered with us to hear. "I wanted to do something that would honor our fathers, and also let our friends honor any loved ones they've lost."

"I love that you want to include everyone."

"I do," I tell him, giving him a kiss before I turn back to the guests. "Everyone, please join us in the front of the house. We are going to light lanterns and send them into the sky for our loved ones who have passed on."

We lead everyone to the front, and light our lanterns first, letting them float out of our hands and into the night sky. My friends all do the same. The Corrigans light theirs together, and then I see Matt light another one, and I know it is for the man he accidentally killed. Reina wraps her arms around him as he lets it go. It's a beautiful sight, the sea of lanterns floating through the air. Gavin turns me to him, and kisses me again. "Beautiful."

"They are."

"I meant you."

"Oh, well thank you."

"Candi's motioning us over for pictures, and then we can have dinner."

"I can't wait. I'm sure your students did justice to our recipes."

"They did. I checked in on them before I got dressed."

"I'm sure you did," I say with a laugh, as we walk over to join the rest of the wedding party.

We take our pictures while the guests inside enjoy some appetizers, and a traditional lion dance. I change into my red gown, and Candi takes candid pictures of us as we walk in to cheers. The lion leads us to our table for two. Our friends and my family are seated around us, but there are too many to include at one table. Gavin really wanted it to be just the two of us, and after driving him crazy over the wedding, I wasn't going to argue with him over this. Especially since eating between us is always very intimate, no matter where we are.

When the waiter brings us each two glasses of beer instead of the wine we picked for dinner, I shoot Gav a quizzical look. "I have a surprise for you."

"Beer?"

"A special meal. Just for us. And yes, beer."

The plates are brought out a couple of minutes later, and it all becomes clear to me. These glasses of beer aren't just any drink. They're our fathers' favorite drinks. To go along with the orange duck that my father loved, and the shepherd's pie that Gavin's told me was his father's favorite.

"You…you cooked this for us, didn't you?" I ask, as tears fall down my face.

"Your grandfather helped. You did things to make sure their presence was known to everyone. I wanted to do the same, just for us."

"It's…thank you. I love you so much, Gav."

"You're welcome, and it's a good thing you love me, because you're stuck with me forever."

"Beyond forever, my love."

We kiss to more cheers, but I tune them out as I think of nothing but Gavin and how he knows what I need, even before I do. Our relationship may have started out with lies and secrets, but now we have love, and a life together. I can't wait to see what comes next.

STELLA & KACE

<u>Stella</u>

"You need to tell Kace," Tegan says to me as I turn from side to side in my lace, strapless, mermaid style gown.

"Not yet."

"He's going to find out. You can't keep what you're doing a secret from him forever."

"Well, duh. He'll know in two weeks."

"As your best friend, I really need to tell you again that this is a bad idea. I know you think it's romantic, and it is, but I don't think he'll see it that way."

"Of course he'll see it that way. He loves me."

"He does, Stell, but this may be too much. Just tell him how you feel. What you want."

"What if he doesn't want it?"

"I highly doubt that, but even if it's true, wouldn't it be better to find that out now?"

"No. He won't embarrass me in front of our friends and family, so it's perfect to wait until then."

"Seriously? You want him to marry you just to avoid embarrassment? Honey, no."

"Of course I don't want that. He'll marry me because he wants to."

My phone rings, cutting off any further Debbie Downer sentiments from my bestie. It'll all work out. It has to. I pick up the phone and smile when I see Kace's picture flash on the screen. Or rather a picture of Kace's abs, shark tattoo and all.

"Hi, K."

"Stella, why did my publicist just tell me that there's reports of us getting married in two weeks. And more importantly, why did your mom practically run from the room when I turned to ask her if she knew anything."

He sounds pissed, and now I'm a little scared. I still try to make the best of it. "Surprise."

There's silence on the line for almost a full minute, and I sit on the edge of a chair in my office, not sure I can stand, but not wanting to fall and ruin my dress. I don't think he's going to say anything, but then I hear a sigh, and he's talking to me again.

"You told me not to ask you to marry me, that you liked things the way they are, and now you're planning a wedding?"

"Yes."

"You need to stop planning this; we need to talk. There's a flight to Vegas in two hours. I'll be on it."

"I'll pick you up."

"Don't. You can meet me at the hotel."

"Hotel? Kace, you're scaring me."

"Good, because you've fucking pulled the rug right out from under me. And yes, a hotel. I can't stay with you right now."

"I'm sorry. I'll cancel everything. You don't have to marry me..."

"We'll talk when I get there. I love you, Stell."

"I love you, too."

I drop my phone to the floor and bury my head in my hands. "He hates me."

"Are you kidding? That boy loves you more than anything. He's just angry, and well, I hate to say 'I told you so,' but I did."

"I know. I KNOW!"

I messed up big time, and now it could cost me everything. I have to convince Kace not to walk away from me. There's no other choice, and no other man, for me. He's it, and I need to let him know that and then cancel all of the stupid plans I made for a surprise wedding he doesn't want.

As long as I have him, I don't care about the wedding. I just need him to stay.

* * *

<u>Kace</u>

I texted Stella with my room number when I checked in, and now I'm waiting for her. I'm actually surprised she wasn't already here in the lobby. I appreciate that she's trying to give me some space after what she did. Which in all honestly, is pretty romantic. Or at least it would've been if we were engaged. But she didn't want that. Or at least that's what she told me. Now I don't know what the hell she wants, and that worries me more than a surprise wedding ever could.

The knock at the door has me planting my feet instead of running to it, like I normally would. I really am scared to know what's going through that beautiful mind of hers, and why it's so important and necessary for us to get married all of a sudden. She knocks again, softer this time when most people would knock harder the second time. She knows I'm in here, and I'm pretty sure she's scared, too. That's what makes me move. No matter what, I love Stella more than life itself. I have to stand up for myself, but I won't intentionally cause her any pain.

I open the door to see her in sweats and a t-shirt, her hair in a messy bun. The last time I saw her like this, she

Society Weddings • 43

was keeping things from me. Things that tore us apart before we fought to put ourselves back together again. We haven't kept things from each other since then, and I vow that tonight will be no different. She needs to tell me what's going on.

"Come in, love," I say, purposely using my nickname for her.

"I'm sorry, K. Really sorry."

She bursts into tears, and I pull her into the room, and into my arms. "I know. It's going to be okay."

"I messed up," she says to my chest.

"You did, but it's nothing we can't fix."

She looks up at me then. "You mean it?"

"Of course I mean it. Let's sit down, and you can tell me why you need us to get married all of a sudden."

"Okay."

I lead her to the couch, and sit us down, pulling her onto my lap. She looks surprised, but then smiles at me and puts her head on my shoulder. "Talk to me."

"I've been helping plan everyone's weddings."

"And doing an amazing job, I might add."

"Thanks."

"So tell me, what made you change your mind about marriage?"

"I was at lunch last week with the girls, and they were all talking about being Mrs. now or becoming Mrs. All of a sudden it hit me that I wanted to be Mrs. Kace Reynolds.

It sounded so right in my head that I felt it all the way to my bones. I didn't even think—I just started planning our wedding. Surprising you seemed like such a good idea. Tegan tried to tell me to call you, but I just thought I was being romantic. Until I wasn't."

"You're romantic, love. I was just shocked, because I didn't think you wanted to get married. You said over and over that you didn't."

"And you don't. I know."

"No. You don't know. I want to marry you. Hell, I've probably always wanted to marry you. I just didn't want to push you into something you weren't interested in."

"You've let me hurt you all this time, and didn't say a word."

"You weren't hurting me. Well, except for that time with the candle wax, but my abs and I survived that."

"I just planned something small. I don't know how it got out."

"Some idiot spilled it, but we have a problem if you were planning small."

"Why?"

"You once told me that if you ever did decide to get married, you wanted the biggest wedding of all."

"Oh yeah. Well I didn't think I could keep it a surprise if it was big."

"Now that you don't need to surprise me anymore, go big, my beautiful bombshell. Whatever you want. Well, except for the bouquet. I saw something online one day, and I want to do it for you."

"My bouquet?"

"Yep."

"Okay. You're sure about this? All of it?"

"Marrying you and wanting you to have the big wedding of your dreams? Yes, I'm sure. In fact, it's about time I finally gave you something."

I sit her on the couch, and then go to my knees in front of her as I pull the ring from my pocket. I've had this ring for over a year, and I can't even describe how happy I am to finally put it on Stella's finger. She yelps, and covers her mouth with her hands.

"Stella, I think I've loved you since you told me you didn't play with little boys. I worked hard to prove to you that age doesn't matter, and I would do it all again. Okay, well, not all of it, but most. Like the bowling alley. We need to go play there again. Anyway, I would love nothing more than to spend the rest of my life being able to call you Mrs. Reynolds. Will you please marry me?"

"Yes."

"Thank God."

I open my palm to let her see the five carat princess cut diamond surrounded by a band of smaller diamonds that I chose for her. "It's perfect. I love it. Oh, Kace. I love you."

"I love you, too," I tell her as I slide that ring on the finger it belongs to.

"I was sad that you didn't want to come home to me, but that bed looks pretty nice."

"You wanna see if we can break it?" I ask with a smirk as she nods.

We've broken more hotel beds than I can count. And I didn't mind paying for them one damn bit. Every single one was worth it. Just like she's worth it. Always.

* * *

<u>Stella</u>

Today is finally the day. My day. Our day. I'm marrying Kace today, becoming Mrs. Reynolds. It's amazing what you can put together in two weeks when you have no budget, and a rolodex filled with famous and influential friends. Add a few more rolodexes to the mix, nine to be exact, and yeah, magic happens.

I'm in my lace mermaid gown, with my hair in an intricate updo, and a veil hanging down my back. The girls are all in green ball gowns, neon green for nine of them, and emerald green for Tegan. That hair of hers would've clashed with the lighter color, and she wouldn't dye it for me despite my pleas, so I relented and had a special one created for her. They all look like princesses with the tulle and taffeta strapless gowns, and that's exactly what I wanted. I'm no princess, but that doesn't mean my girls can't be.

The only thing I'm nervous about now is my bouquet. Kace said it would be delivered before the ceremony, and I'm still waiting. Logically, I know my mom will be bringing it to me once she's done getting him and the other guys dressed, but I'm still anxious. Everyone else has white roses, which I picked because they are classic and classy, and also so they'd match whatever I'm getting.

"I believe you need a bouquet," she says, gliding into the room, looking like a glamorous movie star from the Fifties in her pale green dress. She has a box in her hand, and I eagerly take it from her.

I practically tear off the ribbon, and throw off the top. What I see steals my breath away. Kace didn't just get me a bouquet, he got me the *perfect* bouquet. It's not made of flowers, but rather antique diamond brooches. Some are shaped like flowers, while others are butterflies or just swirls of diamonds.

"Oh. My. God."

"That boy of yours did good. He found them all on line himself. He even tried to put them together into the bouquet, but I had to step in."

"Thanks, Mom. I can't believe he did this."

"He loves you."

"I love him, too. So much. I was scared I was going to lose him when I was so stupid about this wedding."

"You didn't give him enough credit."

"I know. It's just I worry that things are too perfect between us. I feel like we can't really be this happy forever."

"Why not? You've found your forever, Stella. Stop fighting it, and just embrace what you have."

"Thanks for the pep talk."

"That's what you keep me around for."

"I love you, Mom."

"And I love you, my beautiful girl. Now let's go get you married."

Because we're having such a grand wedding, I asked for permission to use the grounds at our apartments. We don't usually let anyone but our closest friends and family in, but this is the most secure building I know of anywhere, and Ainsley and Scott were able to block all camera, and satellite feeds. Reina got the space over us declared a no-fly zone, and now I'm about to walk down the aisle to my pop star without the eyes of the world on us. Just the 300 invited guests. I won't win the contest for grandest since that title belongs to Reina for her televised affair. She hated every second of it, and honestly, I'm just fine with the way this wedding has turned out. Being Mrs. Reynolds means more to me than any wedding ever could.

When the girls have gone before me, I stop at the large circular window that looks out onto the grounds, and smile. This is right. I may have thought I didn't want marriage and kids, but I want both. Not all at once, but soon.

First, I need to take the hand my mom has outstretched towards me, and walk down the aisle.

I'm halfway down the aisle when I decide that patience is definitely not a virtue I have. I give my mom a quick kiss on the cheek, reach down for the hem of my dress, and sprint the rest of the way. Four inch heels be damned, I want my man. The one who's looking oh so sexy in a black suit with a matching vest, and no tie. I am a lucky, lucky woman.

He's laughing as he hops down the two steps to meet me. "Couldn't wait, love?"

"For you? Never."

I lean up and kiss him, causing the guests to laugh, and Wayne, who got ordained online just so he could marry us, to clear his throat loudly. Several times. We finally break apart to see him glaring at us.

"Look, I didn't go through the boot camp like hurdles I did to get this license just to have the two of you blatantly disregard the sanctity of this wedding."

"You clicked a few buttons on the website, asshole," Kace tells him. "That's hardly boot camp."

"My fingers are precious."

"You're precious, alright."

"Just take your damn places, please."

We smile at each other, before doing as he asks. The rest of the ceremony goes as expected. When I promise to obey him, Kace's eyes go dark. I smirk at him, and lick my lips, knowing full well we're going to end up late to our own wedding reception. Our guests will understand.

* * *

Kace

It's nearly killing me to stand and take pictures after the wedding. Don't get me wrong, I love being photographed with Stella and our friends and family, but hiding a hard on while standing next to your parents is not fun. When Stella moves in front of me, I think she's helping me out. Until she rubs that perfect ass of hers over my cock.

"Payback's a bitch, love," I whisper in her ear.

"Good thing I like it rough," She whispers back.

"You're not helping my…*situation*."

"Poor baby boy, do you need me to kiss it and make it better?"

I groan in her ear. Who am I kidding? That groan was loud enough to be heard two states over. "The thought of you on your knees in that wedding dress while you suck me off …holy hell…I want that so fucking bad."

"As your wife, it's my job to make sure *all* of your needs are met," she says, and then turns to everyone else. "I think we have enough pictures for now. Why don't you all head on in to cocktail hour. Faith and Gavin have really outdone themselves."

"Aren't you two heading in?" my mom asks her.

"Soon. I need Kace's help with something first." Fuck yeah she does.

Tegan smirks at us both before leaning in like she's hugging us. "I'll hold everyone off, but I can't do it indefinitely. Go get your freak on."

We don't have to be told twice. Once everyone has gone into the reception tent, I lead her inside our building, and down to the bowling alley. When we walk in and she sees the candles all over, she pulls me to a stop and kisses me. I want to strip her bare, and fuck her hard, but I haven't forgotten her earlier promise. I lead us to the lane I set up and drop a pillow to the floor. She pushes me down into one of the seats with a smile.

I watch her sink to her knees, causing her tits to almost pop out of the top of her dress. I reach out and run my hands over the exposed skin while she unzips my pants, and pulls my dick out of my briefs. "You're so beautiful, Stella."

"That's Mrs. Reynolds to you."

"Well then, Mrs. Reynolds, please put my cock in your mouth before I die."

"Since you asked so nicely," she says, kissing me once, and then taking me deep into her mouth.

I watch her for about a minute, enjoying the view. I love seeing my cock go in and out of her mouth almost as much as I love seeing it go in and out of her pussy. I try to hold on, but she knows exactly what to do to make me come hard. One squeeze of my balls, and some stroking to go with the sucking, and yeah, I drop my head back and yell out her name as I empty myself down her throat.

I take a moment to come back down to Earth as she places kisses on my abs and ribs. I know taking me in her mouth made her even hornier than she was earlier. Giving me pleasure turns her on, just like eating her pussy does the same to me. And that pussy of hers is next on the menu.

I stand up, and then help her to her feet, unzipping her dress, but catching it before it falls to the ground. We'll have to go back eventually, and I know she'll want her dress to come out of all of this unscathed. I set it on the chairs and turn back to her. And nearly have a heart attack.

Without her dress, she's in just a tiny white satin strapless bra, and sheer, lace topped, stockings. No panties. No fucking panties. If I'd known that earlier, I would've never made it through the pictures.

But the most beautiful thing she's wearing, by far, is a smile. "Thank you for taking care of my dress."

"Welcome," I say taking her hand and pulling her over to the bowling ball return.

"I did enjoy this last time," she reminds me.

"You don't honestly think we're doing the same thing, do you? I mean, come on, you don't see me as a one-trick pony, do you?"

"If I lie and say yes, do I get to ride you?"

"Later. Now straddle the fan."

She does as I ask, but she's not exactly where I need her. I move her forward a little, take off her shoes so she's lower, and then drop to my knees. As the hot air hits her center, I take my first lick. Stella starts moving her hips as the stream of hot air combines with my mouth to bring her close to the edge.

"Fuck, Kace."

"Soon," I say. "After you come on my tongue."

I lick lower, feeling the heat on my tongue as I plunge it in and out of her. Alternating between her sweet little clit, and her dripping pussy, I take her over the edge as she screams.

"Ready for your ride now, love?"

"Yes. Please yes."

I lean back and pull her on top of me. We don't need fancy for this, just a good old-fashioned fucking. She slides down my cock, and then we're both moving. I pull her tits out of the bra, and feast on them while she rides me hard and fast. We're both so far gone that it only takes minutes before she's shuddering, and I'm coming right behind her. Once we're both momentarily satisfied, I start to laugh.

"What's so funny?"

"I didn't even realize you still had your veil on until now."

"What? Oh, shit. I didn't realize it either."

"I almost wish we didn't have to go back, but they'll be looking for us soon."

"We have the rest of our lives together to do this over and over again."

"Yes, we do."

We get up, and put ourselves back together. We're holding hands as we enter the tent. I see the cool, modern chandeliers she placed at every table, and she sees my next surprise. I had Swarovski encrusted letters spelling "Mr.," "&", and "Mrs." placed in the middle of the dance floor.

"I love them. Oh wow. I want them in the apartment."

"Whatever you want."

"I want you. Today…the bouquet…the vest…the sex…the letters…you've made this day perfect for me."

"The vest comes before the sex?"

She rolls her eyes. "I wasn't listing things in order, horn-dog."

"Just checking. And for the record, today was perfect for me, too. After all, I got to marry you, Mrs. Reynolds."

"Ditto, Mr. Reynolds. Ditto."

ISA & JAKE

<u>Jake</u>

"You holding up okay?" I ask Isa, walking into her office at the Corrigan & Co. Foundation.

"Sure. Why wouldn't I be? I mean, your mother has just taken over my wedding, and now one of your ex-girlfriends has turned up dead, only to have her father hire us to find out who killed her. And let's not forget that you're his number one suspect."

"No one believes I killed Skylar. And even if they did, I have an airtight alibi. I was servicing my fiancé that night, and the apartment cameras will prove I never left the building."

"I know. Logically, I know that. I just worry."

I move behind her to massage her shoulders. "Don't worry about that. We're good there. Now tell me what my mother's done now."

"The usual. She thinks this is her wedding."

"I'll take care of her."

"No, Jake. It's fine. It's just a wedding, right? I mean, being married is more important."

I step around to lean on her desk and look at my sweet girl. "Yes, marriage is the most important thing, but that doesn't mean that you shouldn't have your dream wedding."

"Even if it's silly?"

"What could possibly be silly about your dreams?"

"What I want isn't sensible, or sophisticated."

"Good. Those two things are highly overrated."

"So you'd be okay if you walked into a wedding and reception full of pink, pearls, and maybe a little bling? Nothing as sparkly as Stella's, but I think I'd like a little."

"I'd even dress in pink if that's what you want."

"No," she says with a laugh. "Maybe slate grey?"

"That works, too."

"Now, I just need to convince your mother."

"No. I said I'd handle her, and I will. You just go ahead and plan what you want."

"She wants to be involved. I think that's a good thing."

"She can be involved as long as she supports you, and what you want."

"You don't have to do this. I should just stand up for myself."

"Isabelle Carlton, you are one of the strongest women I know, but my mother is…well, you know how she is. Standing up to her is work. A lot of work you don't need. She won't give me any trouble."

"Thank you."

"No need to thank me. Just keep loving me forever, and we'll call it even."

"Deal."

I kiss her softly, which turns into more than kissing. Just like it always does. She finally tells me I have to leave so she can work on Skylar's murder investigation. I'd like to have this case closed before the wedding, so I don't put up much of a fight.

I "dated" Skylar years ago. I use that term loosely because it was more like we were each other's arm candy, and we had sex a few times. End of story. At least until news of my upcoming wedding to Isa broke. For some reason Sky wanted her fifteen minutes of fame and tried to use us to get it. She'd been all over the media for weeks claiming that we'd been having a clandestine affair, and that I was going to dump Isa at the altar. Never mind that I would never touch another woman, but the times she said I was with her were times I was with Isa and our friends. Even in D.C., I was either with Aiden or Vicki. Isa knows this and told me from the beginning that she'd never believe I cheated on her, but I still wish I understood why Sky did it. I guess I'll never know now.

I do know one thing, though. My mother needs to be reined in. I call her as I get into the elevator.

"Darling, I didn't expect to hear from you so soon. Did something happen with Skylar's case?"

"No. Something happened with my wedding. I need you to stop trying to run over Isa. She's either going to have the wedding of her dreams, or I'm taking her to the drive-thru chapel. Without you."

"You wouldn't."

"After all that's happened, you really believe I wouldn't do everything in my power to make sure Isa's every wish and dream comes true?"

"When you put it that way, I guess not. I was only trying to help your image, you know. A sophisticated affair would go a long way in this town."

"When have I ever cared about my image?"

"Never. Fine, it was about me."

"When it's really supposed to be about Isa."

"And you. Don't you want anything?"

"Yes. I want the woman I love to be happy. That's all I need or want."

"I'll be nice."

"I know you will, because you know I'm not kidding about the drive-thru chapel."

"I shouldn't have raised you to be so tough. It's coming back to bite me in the ass."

"Karma, Mom. Karma. It'll get you every time."

* * *

<u>Isa</u>

I've been going over the details for Skylar's murder, and nothing is jumping out at me. I have that nagging feeling in my brain telling me I'm missing something, but for the life of me, I don't know what. Maybe I need to step away and wait for Tegan to tell me what she sees. We purposely stay away from each other for the first day or two of analysis so that we don't influence each other's initial findings.

I'm restless; worrying about finding this killer, and worrying that I'm going to make a mess of my wedding. I probably should've just let Liz Mason give me sophisticated and fancy, but I really want romantic and pink. Ever since Jake talked to her, she's been more than happy to listen to me. I don't know what he said to scare her, but whatever it was, it definitely worked.

She's not a bad person. In fact, if she loves you, she'd slay a zombie for you. And I know she loves me. It's only because Jake does, but still, she loves me. She just likes to project a certain image, and dresses that look like cotton candy don't fit into her mold. But she's breaking her mold for me, and I really appreciate it.

She's canceled the country club and booked the Library of Congress Great Hall, which is where I really wanted to get married. Well, honestly, I wanted to get married at the Smithsonian, but they can't do weddings there. She's also Skyped me in with her florist and smiled indulgently when I picked the pinks and whites with fake diamonds dripping down for my centerpieces. The bridesmaid's dresses were a little harder for her to swallow. They don't really look like cotton candy, just pale pink ruffles with white daisies all over the strapless bodice and scattered around the skirt. I'm not much of a daisy fan, but I fell in love with the dresses, and while Liz doesn't exactly love them, she didn't put out another hit on me. At least not that I know of. As a whole, it's all coming together. Even with the publicity surrounding Skylar's death and fake claims about Jake.

"Hey, girlie," Tegan says from my office doorway. "Are you ready to compare notes?"

"Hey. Yes, I'm more than ready. I keep thinking I missed something."

"I may have your missing something. In fact, I'm pretty sure I do."

"Do tell," I say, leading her to the round table in my office.

"Don't start without me. I helped," Ainsley says, coming in and taking her own seat.

"You did. Isa, what I think I've figured out is that if it hadn't been Skylar, it would've been you. Or at least the murderer would've tried to kill you."

"What? Why?" I ask; although, I think I know.

"Jake. Skylar was murdered after she said they'd been having an affair. Ainsley helped me go through blogs and message boards—there are a disturbing amount of those things dedicated to your man, by the way."

"I know. Back on track, please."

"Anyway, an anonymous person has been posting everywhere about how Jake is hers."

"Anonymous? You haven't found the identity yet?" I ask Ainsley.

"No. Whoever is posting has been using different university computers. I've even considered that it's more than one person based on the fact that none of the schools are near each other."

"Why did I have to fall in love with the man every woman in D.C. and the surrounding states wants for herself?"

"Because he's a great guy, and worships the ground you walk on," Ainsley says.

"And don't forget the medal she gave him," Tegan adds with a smirk.

"No one is ever going to forget that medal," I say, shaking my head. Damn boys and their prizes.

Now we just need to figure out who wants Jake enough to kill for him. Because if some bitch tries to mess with my wedding, I will take her down. I have enough stress as it is.

* * *

<u>Jake</u>

"Hey, Vick," I say, answering the phone with a smile.

"It's not your little piece on the side," a male voice that sounds familiar answers.

"Who is this? And why do you have my best friend's phone?"

"Best friend? Yeah, right. Your cheating is catching up on you."

"I don't cheat. And I'm asking you again, who the hell are you?"

"Your judge, jury, and executioner all rolled into one."

"You killed Skylar? Why?"

"If you want to know the answer to that, and maybe save your *friend*, you'll fly to D.C. and meet with me."

"Where in D.C.?"

"You'll get instructions when you land. And come alone. I'll know if you bring anyone."

He hangs up, and I immediately call Matt. Within minutes, a Corrigan jet is ready for me, and Nate, Aiden, and Theo have all headed out to board another one. I won't involve Isa, even though I know she can handle herself. This guy wants me, and he's going to get me. I had no feelings for Skylar, but Vicki's my best friend. He put his hands on her, and now he's going to die.

I send Isa a text saying that I have to go to D.C. to take care of something. She wishes me a safe trip, trusting that I'll explain it to her later. Which I will. The secrets I kept from her nearly destroyed us both, so I keep nothing from her anymore. Well, almost nothing. I ordered something from "our" jewelry store for her to wear on our wedding day, but she won't know that until Stella gives it to her. Some things need to be a surprise.

The flight is smooth, but my mind is still at war with itself. The voice on the phone was so damn familiar, but as hard as I try, I just can't place it. I know that voice is the key to this puzzle, but the more I think about it, the more it escapes me.

Literally the minute I step into the private terminal, my phone rings. "I'm here."

"Such a good little soldier. Too bad you won't be rewarded."

"Just tell me where you are, motherfucker."

He tells me in a scolding tone, and I don't hesitate to go. I pick up a rental car, acting as if I'm just booking it, when in reality, it's been arranged for me. The gun is right where Nate told me it would be under the dashboard, and the sunglasses with the comm built in are on the front seat. Theo is in charge of ground support, because working for

Aiden's dad gave him information on all the ins and outs of the city.

I drive to the location, praying that I'll find my best friend still alive. Vicki and I have had our ups and downs, but she's still the person I'm closest to, besides Isa. They're super close now, too, which means I'm totally going to get hell for not including her on this. I couldn't take a chance with either of them, and I hope they both understand that.

I've got to keep up the pretense that I'm not hiding anything—namely the gun strapped to my ankle—so I walk right in the front door of the converted warehouse I was sent to. It looks like it's being remodeled into a home, but I don't get too much time to look around. I hear shuffling behind me, and turn to see Vicki being pulled into the room by Creed McCall. Yeah, the TV star half the women on this planet are in lust with. Now I know why his voice sounded familiar.

"Hello, Jake."

"Have we met?"

"No. But you've taken something that should've been mine."

"I'm not sure what that could be."

"Not what, who. Isa. She was supposed to be mine."

In what alternate universe would that have happened? "Does she know that?"

"No. I was trying to take things slow while she was protecting me. I was being her friend."

"She's a very friendly woman," I concede.

"I was getting ready to take the next step and ask her out. Then you came along."

"I'm not sorry, man. I mean, I get why you'd hate to lose her, but killing people is not the answer."

"I want to kill you, but it would break Isa's heart, and I don't want her like that. I need her whole. Killing your sluts will make her realize just who you really are, and send her running to me when I call."

"She knows I'm faithful to her. I hadn't touched Skylar in years, and Vicki's my best friend. She's one of Isa's best friends now, too."

"No! This is my plan, and it will work the way I want it to."

His crazy train is going full throttle right now, and I don't know how to stop it without getting Vicki shot. I'm looking for a solution that I don't end up needing.

"Put the gun down, Creed," Isa says, leveling her own gun at him as she walks in the room from another entrance.

"Isa. You're not supposed to be here."

"But I am, and you're going to let my friend go."

"She's not your friend. She wants him."

"No, she doesn't. And even if she did, he only wants me. And I only want him."

"He can't love you like I can."

"He loves me exactly how I need him to. Now put the gun down, or you'll force me to shoot you."

"You wouldn't."

"I would."

He pushes Vicki away, and then raises his gun to his head. I shoot the gun out of his hand before he has a chance to save himself from prison. "You're going to jail today, asshole, not the morgue."

The police rush in and take him. Vicki gets checked out while I pull Isa aside. I know she's pissed at me because she thinks I came alone, so I brace myself.

"Are you insane?"

"No."

"You came alone to meet with a murderer?"

"No."

"No?"

"Aiden, Nate, and Theo are here."

"Oh. You still should've told me."

"I know how much stress you're under with the wedding and everything. I was going to tell you when I got back."

"*If* you got back. What if he'd killed you?"

"We wouldn't have let that happen Double G," Nate says, enveloping her in a hug.

"I guess not. You're really taking the wind out of my sails, you know. I was all ready to be angry."

"You can knock me around later when we're alone," I tell her, pulling her into my arms.

"Don't tempt me."

"Okay, and that's our cue to leave," Theo says. "Catch you guys back in Vegas."

"Thanks for coming with me."

"Anytime, man. We can't let our women have all the fun," Aiden says with a smirk.

"How did you figure it out?" I ask her when they're gone.

"Tegan thought it was a woman who wanted you, but when she mentioned college campuses being used to post things, something clicked. I remembered seeing that Creed would be touring college campuses as part of some reality show. I know I'm naïve, but I could tell he wanted more than friendship. He got really angry when I told him I was seeing you. Ainsley traced him to D.C., and when you said you were coming here, I knew something was up."

"You tracked me, didn't you?"

"Yes, and aren't you glad I did?"

"I had everything under control," I lie. She raises an eyebrow at me. "Or maybe not."

"You're lucky I love you Jake Mason."

"I am very aware of that fact, Isabelle Carlton."

* * *

Isa

I look at myself in the mirror and can't believe this day has finally come. I look like a princess with my dress that has a high lace back, but still gives me a little cleavage with the straight neckline in the front. The bodice is satin covered in lace, and the skirt is organza layers that flare from my hips to the ground, making me look like I stepped out of a fairytale. My hair is in a loose bun with some curls hanging down, and I opted for no veil. I'm reaching for my pearl necklace when Stella stops me.

"Jake left this for you," she tells me, handing me a jewelry box.

I open it to see yet another gorgeous piece of jewelry from my man. This one is a strand of diamonds forming a bow and then curving up to surround a giant light pink stone. "What kind of gem is this?"

"I don't know. Do you really care?"

"Not at all. It's gorgeous."

"It is. So is Jake. He's smoking in his suit."

"If anyone else was saying that to me, I'd slap them."

"You know I'm not looking at him like that."

"Exactly."

"Are you ready?" Vicki asks, handing me my bouquet. It's got pink and white roses and peonies, and a sparkly handle thing. There's probably a specific name for it, but I don't care enough to ask. Which is weird for me, but hey, I'm getting married today.

"I am. You can go take your place with Jake."

"Thanks for letting me get ready with all of you and wear one of these dresses. I wasn't on board with the idea of wearing a tux." She's Jake's "best woman", so I wanted her to feel like part of the wedding party instead of wearing something else.

"Of course. You know I love you."

"I love you, too. I never thought Jake would have a woman in his life who would accept our friendship, but I'm glad he found you."

"Me too."

Everyone lines up, and they start walking out. Our ceremony is happening in the Reading Room, which fits less people than the Grand Hall. Jake and I only want our friends and family with us for this part. The rest of the guests his mother invited can join us for the reception, but this is our day, and we're doing it our way. Well, mostly my way, but I have asked Jake about everything, and I even let him pick the cake flavor. Chocolate with cream cheese frosting—no surprise from him there.

We flew in the Drago sisters, and Eliza. They used a rented kitchen to make the cake for us. No Society woman will be married without a cake from them. The idea of it is absurd to us. Over the years, they've become friends as well as our bakers. Having them as part of our days is a given.

Gary Griffin offers me his arm, and we make our way into the room. Stella wasn't kidding. Jake looks hot in his formal suit and pink tie. He's got a big smile on his face, which makes me realize that he likes what he's seeing as well. We reach him, and Gary gives him my hand.

The Supreme Court Justice who's officiating says all the words, and we say our "I Do's." We place our identical bands on each other's fingers, looking at the secret messages from each other on the inside of them. The outside is platinum, and has both of our fingerprints with an "&" symbol in between. We found them online, and they're perfect for us. I love my pink diamond, but the band is more practical for my day to day life.

Jake dips me down into a dramatic kiss as everyone claps. "I finally made an honest woman of you, Mrs. Mason."

"Honesty is the best policy, Mr. Mason."

"I love you, Isa. More than anything."

"I love more than anything, too, Jake. Thank you for making all of my dreams come true."

"It's been my pleasure. And it's going to be yours once we can get away later."

"Not mine. Ours. Always ours."

"Yes, Forever ours, my love."

TEGAN & *CALEB*

<u>Caleb</u>

"You're sure pink is okay? Isa had a pink wedding. Is it too soon after for ours to be pink, too?"

Stella looks at me like I've lost my mind. "Teeg loves pink. It doesn't matter if your weddings were on the same day. We'd need to go pink."

"Yeah, okay. I just want this all to be perfect."

"I'm planning it, aren't I?"

"Were you ever humble? I mean, as a kid?"

"Maybe. I don't know. There's nothing wrong with being confident."

"I guess."

"Do I intimidate you with my awesomeness, Caleb?"

Yes. "No. You're my wife's best friend. Why would I be intimidated by you?"

"Maybe because I remember the names you called her, and I'll cut off your dick if you ever do that again."

My dick wants me to retreat now, and hide, but Stella can sense fear. All of the Society women can. I raise my chin and look her in the eye. "We both know that will never happen again."

"Yes, we do. Now stop worrying about the color pink, and let's get the rest of this stuff finalized."

"Yes, ma'am."

Our fourteen-month wedding anniversary is coming up this weekend, and it's past time that I give Tegan the wedding she's always dreamed of. She says she's just happy we're married, but I know the wedding chapel isn't what she'd always hoped for. For a long time, I wasn't the guy she'd hoped for, but now I am. She doesn't expect anything from me except me, but I want her to have everything I can give her. Starting with this wedding. Her dream wedding by our creek.

"I don't have to wear pink, do I? I mean, I love Mama, but I have a rep to protect," Ethan says, speaking up from behind my desk where he's been doing his homework.

"A rep? Really, E?"

"Yeah. I'm cool."

"Ooh, are the little teeny girls wanting to get busy with you?" Stella asks.

"Shut it, Stell," I warn her with a glare.

"They are," he tells her, ignoring me. "I got five numbers today."

"You are way too young for that shit."

"I'm almost thirteen. Don't worry, Dad. I'll cover my snake when the time comes."

"Oh. My. God," Stella says, nearly falling off the chair as she laughs. "Snake? Have you not had the talk with him?"

"I have. And you're more than half a year from being thirteen, so keep it in your damn pants."

"I know how it works," he says. "I won't take it out until I'm ready."

"Baby boy, if you think you're man enough to be using it, you should be calling it what it is. No girl wants to hear your dick referred to as a snake. None. Trust me on this."

"Is that what you call it, Dad?"

Kill me now. Or rather, kill Stella. I know she's Teeg's BFFL, but she needs to rein it in with our pre-teen son. He's still looking at me for an answer, and I know he's not going to let it go. I glare at Stella before answering.

"Sometimes."

"What do you call it the rest of the time?"

"We'll talk about this later."

"Why? I mean, you're not embarrassed to have me here while you talk about your 'love member' are you?"

"Who the hell calls it that? Kace?"

"Yeah, no."

"Come on Dad, just tell me."

"Cock," I mumble.

"Like a gun?"

Stella falls off the chair that time. She's on the floor holding her stomach when Tegan walks in. "What's going on?"

"Dad was telling me how he calls his wiener a cock. Like a gun."

"Excuse me?"

"It's her fault," I say, pointing at Stella.

"Don't act like you don't love it when he cocks his gun for you, Teeg."

"Kill me now," I say with a groan.

"I just might," Tegan says. "I fucking just might."

* * *

<u>Tegan</u>

I've been freezing Caleb out for a couple of days now. Stella and Ethan told me it wasn't his fault, but he's the most adult of the three, and he should've known better than to get sucked into that conversation. Our anniversary is tomorrow, though, and I'm planning to let him back into our bed tonight. I know most people don't celebrate every month, but we do. We're so happy to be back together after so long that we celebrate as much as we can. I have the perfect gift for him, and really, I'm punishing myself just as much as him when I make him sleep in the guest room.

"We need to head out," Stella says, coming into my office with a tentative smile on her face. I haven't kept my anger at her a secret, either.

"I have no place to be."

"Actually, you do."

"Where?"

"Texas," Ethan tells me, running into the room and hugging me. "We get to see Grandma and Grandpa."

"What's going on?" I ask.

"I have a surprise for you," Caleb tells me. He's standing outside of the door, and I feel bad that he looks nervous and unsure.

"You can come into my office, you know."

He shrugs. "I know you're angry with me."

"Which is stupid," Ethan tells me.

"Excuse me?"

"I asked Dad about his dick, and he told me. Isn't that what he's supposed to do? Or do you want me just watching porn and thinking that's what sex should be?"

I try hard not to have a panic attack, but my breathing grows heavy. "Have you been watching porn?"

"Not yet. But it's what guys do."

"Not just guys," Stella says.

"Not helping, Stell."

"She is. I want to know everything. You always say a person should know as much as they can so they can make an educated decision. I want to know all about sex, so when the time's right, I'll do it right."

He's right. Darn kid. "I'm not sure we know *everything*, but your Dad and I will tell you what we know."

"Me and Kace too. In fact, I bet everyone would tell you things. Not details about our sex lives, because that would be weird, but we could try to answer your questions."

"Cool. Maybe just the guys, though."

"I think we can arrange that," Caleb says."

"Now that we've settled the sex ed dilemma, can someone please tell me why we're going to Texas?"

"We're getting married," Caleb tells me with a smile.

I grab his left hand with mine and hold them up. "Been there, done that. I've been Mrs. Caleb Hall for over a year."

"We got married in a wedding chapel. Now it's time for the real thing, in the real place."

My mouth drops open, and my heart starts to race again, but in a good way this time. "The creek?"

"Of course."

I launch myself into his arms as I fuse my lips to his. He catches me and holds me in his arms until Ethan starts making gagging noises. We break apart with a laugh. "I need a dress, and flowers, and…"

"It's all taken care of," Stella tells me. "Caleb and I have been working on this for over a month."

"Of course you have. Let's go."

I can't believe Cal is doing this for me. But actually, yeah, I can. Despite me telling him I'm fine with our Vegas wedding, he knows me well enough to know what I really wanted. I'll never regret marrying him when I did, but secretly hoped that one day we could go to the creek and do it all over again. It looks like tomorrow is the day. For his surprise, and mine, too.

* * *

Caleb

"You're really not going to let me see the setup?" Tegan says, running her fingers up and down my t-shirt. She plays dirty, but that's more than fine with me.

"Nope. It wouldn't be a surprise then, would it?"

"But the pier is down there," she reminds me, biting her lip, and moving her hands lower. "We've had some good times at the pier."

"We have," I concede, grabbing her hands and bringing them to my lips. "Very good times. In fact, I'm looking forward to a trip down there tomorrow night."

"What about our guests? We are having guests, aren't we?"

"For a spy, your fishing skills are a little obvious." She smacks my arm, and I pull her close. "Our friends, and my family will be in the barn for the reception."

I realize that was the wrong thing to say. "The barn? Let's go to the loft so you can make me scream."

"And you can see the decorations in there?"

She shrugs. "Don't you want to put your mouth on me and make me scream? It's been so long."

"You're the one who made me sleep in the guest room the last two nights. You missed all of those screaming opportunities."

"I'm not going to win, am I?"

"Not a chance. You'll love everything. I promise."

"I know I will. Between you and Stella, it can only be great."

"Ethan helped, too."

"About him. What are we going to do with all his interest in sex?"

"Just be there when he needs us. He's about to be a teenage boy. Being curious is natural. I'm just glad he wants to know the truth from us."

"I know you're right, but he's my little guy."

"Who's almost as tall as you."

She bursts out crying then. "I don't want him to grow up."

Whoa. I pull her into my arms, and rub her back. "He has to grow up, darlin', you know that. You also know our boy loves you more than anything."

"He loves you too," she says, sniffling into my shirt.

"I know he does." I do know that. We had a rocky start because he thought I would hurt her again, and he'll protect Tegan to the death. Once he realized I would do the same, and I stopped being an ass to her, we've been as close as my own dad and I are.

"I'm a mess."

"Yeah, but you're a sexy mess, and I love you."

"I love you, too."

The doorbell rings, and I smile. "That's your girls. I'll see you tomorrow."

"Wait, what? I was going to let you back into bed with me tonight."

"You're seriously killing me."

"So stay."

"It's the night before our wedding."

"We're already married, and I'm not superstitious."

The doorbell rings again. "Let me do this right for you. Please."

"Fine. Get out of here before I take you to the floor right here."

I kiss her hard and then force myself to run to the door. I let them in and head next door to my parents' ranch. Ethan is waiting for me in the driveway, and I smile at him as I get out of my truck.

"Waiting for your dear old dad?"

"You're not that old yet."

"Thanks, kid."

"Can we go look at everything? Grandpa said we had to wait for you."

"Sure. Let's see what magic Stella made happen."

We see the rows of white chairs when we enter the clearing bordering the creek. There are also some hooked thingies in the ground that I think flowers will be hanging off of. Right in front of the pier is a white structure with white fabric, which is where we'll renew our vows. It's simple, but beautiful.

"Wow. This is perfect. Mama's gonna love it."

"Stella knows what your mom likes."

"So do you. I really like that you're doing this for her."

"I'd do anything for her. And you."

"I believe you. I'm glad you're my dad."

"Me too, E. Me too."

* * *

<u>Tegan</u>

"Am I going to get to see my dress anytime soon?" I ask Stella, pouting a little.

"Yes."

"When?"

"When your hair and makeup is done, Mrs. Impatient."

I stick out my tongue at her, but then turn serious. "Thank you for doing this."

"It was Caleb's idea, and he helped me pick a lot of things."

"You made it happen."

She shrugs. "You're my best friend. Of course I want you to have your dream wedding."

"Just like you did."

"Yep. We're some lucky bitches."

"That we are."

"Hey, no tears yet," Reina says, coming up and enveloping us both in a group hug.

She's got her bridesmaid dress on, and I absolutely love it. It's a deep pink strapless dress that looks like it's made of flowers and petals throughout the fitted top, and short, flared skirt. I look down and start to laugh. "I never thought I'd see the day when Reina Corrigan had cowboy boots on her feet."

"You make me sound like an uptight bitch," she says, laughing along with me.

"Nah. Just classy."

"These boots are classy."

They really are. The bridesmaids are all wearing white and silver cowboy boots. I wonder what Stella has planned for me. If I'm being totally honest, I don't want to wear boots. I did that once, and I had always thought I wanted to do it at the creek, but I don't. I want pretty shoes for the ceremony, and my everyday worn brown boots for the reception. That's my new dream.

"Don't worry, you don't have boots," Stella says with a smile.

"What?"

"I know you better than anyone, except Caleb. You want shoes this time around. Maybe boots later."

She really does know me. "You're the best, Stell."

"Back at ya, Teeg. I think you're ready for your dress."

I stand up as she opens the bag, and pulls out the perfect dress. It's chiffon, yards and yards of white chiffon. The top is strapless and gathered. Actually, nothing on the dress is smooth, with the exception of the dark pink band of satin at the waist. The bottom is swirls of chiffon all the way to the ground. There's a long veil that will flow to the floor as well.

"I love it. I love you. Thank you so much."

"Love you, too."

Stella helps me into everything, having to fight the zipper a little because I've gained a few pounds. She just shakes her head and says she should've measured me. Once the dress and veil are on, I slip into the pink satin shoes she has for me. She hasn't given me any jewelry, and I guess I don't really need it, but I feel like something is missing.

"Looking for this?" she asks, holding up a necklace made up of diamond and gemstone flowers. The flowers are all different colors, and it's just adorable. Obviously expensive, but still sweet.

"Wow. You even got me the perfect jewelry."

"Nope. Your husband got you the perfect jewelry."

"I'm so lucky."

"So is he," Jade tells me, hugging me from behind before putting my veil on for me.

Alex hands me a bouquet of roses, lilies, and wildflowers done in shades of pink, white, and green. "Caleb again?"

"Ethan."

My heart is so full right now. For my guys, my friends, and Caleb's family. I really am lucky, and I'll try my hardest to never take advantage of any of them.

We walk out to the creek, and then I'm walking down the aisle on the arm of Caleb's dad. Ethan is the best man today, and so both of my boys greet me when I reach the end of the aisle.

"Thank you for my flowers, E."

"You're welcome. I love you, Mama."

"I love you, too."

"You look beautiful, Cowgirl."

"It's all the diamonds in the necklace my husband bought me. They're blinding you."

"Nothing outshines you. Happy Anniversary."

"Happy Anniversary."

The ceremony is short, since we're just reaffirming things. One of the stable hands leads our horses to us after we walk back up the aisle. Caleb's mom hands me my boots and I lean on him as I change my footwear. "I like the heels, but I have so many fantasies about you and your boots," he whispers in my ear.

"More?" I ask, because my boots have been used in many places and positions over the last year.

"I don't think I'll ever stop fantasizing about you."

"You say the sweetest things."

"Remember that when I'm rough with you later."

"That's when you're the sweetest."

"Woman," he says in warning.

"Man."

"Get on your horse. We need to go to the reception."

"In the barn. With the hayloft."

"Tegan Hall, get your ass on the damn horse."

I just laugh and do as he says. The guests will be taken back in the carriages they rode in on, but we hold hands as we ride next to each other, just like we've done countless times. I can't wait to see what the barn looks like, but I'm not willing to rush this. Especially when I still have his present to give him.

The barn is nothing short of spectacular. There are branches mixed with twinkling lights wrapping around the support beams, dried pink and white flowers along the loft railings, and white tables all over. There was always a large open area in front where business meetings took place, but the whole place has been taken over for the wedding. I know they took the horses to the auxiliary stable, but I don't know how Stella got it to smell so nice in here.

I don't dwell on it as I go over to look at our cake. Just like everything else, it's perfect. Dark pink with frosting that looks like rope around some layers, and shimmery circles on others. The topper is a statue of a man and a woman on their horses, holding hands like Caleb and I just did.

"Everything is so perfect, Cal."

"Thank God. I wanted it to be that way for you."

"I want to give you your present. Can we go upstairs?"

He looks at me with an eyebrow raised. "I'm not sure we can do that with everyone here. You do like to scream."

"Shut up. That's not what I want to go up there for."

"No?"

"Well, I wouldn't turn it down, but no."

"Okay. Let's go."

Once we get up there, I make him sit down, and then I climb on his lap. "What I have to give you isn't something you can see. Yet."

"That's not cryptic at all."

I take his hand and move it to my stomach. His eyes go wide, and I nod. "Yes. I'm pregnant. Almost two months."

"I…this…next to you and E, this is the best present I could ever receive."

"I love you Caleb Hall."

"And I love you, Tegan Hall. Thank you for the gift of you and our children. I promise to work hard to show you how much I love you for the rest of my life."

"I promise to love you back. Now, I think I saw a mouse, so maybe you should make me scream."

JADE & NATE

<u>Jade</u>

"I got a hold of some more of your fighter friends. They can't wait to come out for the wedding."

"Cool," Nate says. Something in his tone tells me it's not in fact, "cool."

"Is something wrong?"

"No, J. We're good."

He turns and kisses me sweetly, but it doesn't change what I feel. "Do you not want to get married?"

He pauses for so long that I almost take the ring he gave me two months ago off my finger. It doesn't look like a typical engagement ring, and I love it even more because of that. It's got a large, square, chocolate diamond with rows of white diamonds crossing over it, and then flowing into a platinum band. He said I was his forever. Now I'm afraid he's changed his mind.

"I want to marry you," he finally says. "I just…"

"What? Say it, Soldier."

"Nothing. It's nothing," he says, kissing me again in an attempt to get me to drop it.

I *can't* drop it. Something's wrong, and he's not telling me what it is. We've been through so much; I thought there were no more secrets, but I guess I was wrong. Thoughts start to swirl through my head. I imagine prettier and sexier girls. Women who would be more girly than I am, and look better on his arm. Does he want them?

I shake my head to try and clear it as I stand up. No. Nate's not like that. If he says he loves me, then he loves me. Period. He. Loves. Me. And no way would he cheat on me.

If it's not that, then I don't know what it is. I just know that if he won't tell me, I'll go crazy sitting here with him. "I'm going to head out for a little while."

"Where are you going?"

"I honestly don't know. I just need to get away from you right now. We've had too many secrets in the past, and I can't deal with you keeping something from me. I'll calm down, and be back, but it's just better if I go."

"I don't want to hurt you. Telling you will hurt you," he says, coming to stand in front of me.

His eyes are pleading with me to stay, but his mouth won't form the words. We both know that I won't stay unless he tells me what's wrong. I just can't.

"Not telling me is hurting. I'll be back."

"Tonight?"

I reach up to cup his cheek with my hand. "Yes. I'll be back tonight."

"I love you, Angel."

"I love you too, Soldier."

I walk out the door, willing myself to be strong. I'm a strong woman. I can handle whatever he's having trouble with. I thought by now he'd realize that, but apparently he doesn't. I finger the ring absently as I descend to the main floor and then the garage. I'm almost to my car when I realize there's no place I want to go right now. At least no place I can drive to.

I go back to the main floor and head outside. My horse is in the barn, and I need him right now. Nate gave me Cherub, and I know I'll feel his love for me when I'm with my other boy. A horse is no substitute for a good man, but it'll have to do for now.

* * *

Nate

"I fucked up," I tell my friends when they get to my place. I called them for help, because I really need it. I don't know what to do right now.

"Seriously? You're getting married in a week," Aiden reminds me.

"That's kind of the problem."

"Wait. Do you not want to marry Jade?" Darcy asks, looking like she might punch me. She was my friend first, but she loves Jade, too.

"I want to marry her more than anything I've ever wanted in my life."

"You just don't want the wedding," Matt says.

I hang my head, because she's hit the nail right on the head. I love Jade, and I want her to be happy, but I don't think I can go through with this big spectacle she's planning. Every fighter her dad knows, plus my fighter friends, military acquaintances, and Society friends she could track down was invited. I just want it to be me, Jade, our close friends, and her dad. That's it.

"No. I don't."

"Have you told her?" Theo asks me.

"I can't. She's so excited. She wants this wedding."

"I'm pretty sure she wants you a whole hell of a lot more than she wants the wedding. And at least you only have one," Darcy tells me.

"No one's forcing you to marry the prince," I remind her with a smirk.

She flips me off. "I love him. I'll endure a fucking royal wedding, and anything else I need to do in order to be his wife. If this wedding is too much for you, maybe you're not as committed to Jade as you think you are."

I jump out of my chair and get in her face. "I love you, Darce, and I would never hit a woman, but don't you dare ever even suggest that I don't love Jade more than the next breath I'm about to take. I'd do anything for her."

"Anything except for the wedding," Jake says, raising an eyebrow at me.

Fuck. He's right. It's not like she's asking me to take a bullet for her—which I would. She wants to walk down the aisle in a pretty dress, and proclaim her love for me to a few hundred people. What guy wouldn't want his girl to do that? It's time for me to stop letting the ghosts of my past control my future. I need to find Jade, and make this right.

"Okay guys, thanks for the pep talk. I've gotta go."

They all file out except for Darcy. "I'm sorry, Nate. I didn't mean to piss you off. I just needed you to see that you're being an ass about this."

"I know, Darce. I shouldn't have gotten in your face. Thanks. For everything."

"Anytime. Now go get your girl."

"Yes, ma'am."

I will the elevator to go faster, but when it reaches the ground floor, I realize that it's not my car I should be running to. She's not going to go out driving to clear her head. She's going to go hang out with her horse. The one I bought her because she joked about wanting a pony. I shake my head at my stupidity again. I gave her a horse, but I can't give her a wedding. I truly am an idiot sometimes.

I walk into the stable and find her in the stall with Cherub. He's lying down with his legs folded up under him, and she's hugging him as she sobs. I didn't know my heart could hurt any more than it did when she sent me away, but it does now.

Cherub sees me and lets out a neigh, while bearing his teeth to me. Jade's eyes fly open, and they go wide when she sees me. "Behave, Cherub. That's your daddy."

"He's definitely a mama's boy," I say, trying to lighten the mood.

"What are you doing here?" she asks, trying to hide the tears she wipes away.

"I'm sorry."

"For what?"

She needs to hear it, and yeah, I need to say the words. "I didn't want people staring at me."

A look of horror crosses her face, and I know she understands now. "Oh God, Nate. Why didn't you tell me? You should've told me. I knew you were hiding things, and I thought…"

"What did you think, Angel?"

"Honestly, at first, I thought you wanted someone else, but I knew I was wrong. Then I just didn't know what to think. All I could think about was that there were secrets again, and the last secrets nearly destroyed both of us."

"There's no one else. Never anyone else. I'm glad you realized it, but I'm sorry you even thought that for a minute. Or even seconds. I love you so much, J."

"I love you, too. I'm so sorry about the wedding. I should've realized it wouldn't be okay."

"It *is* okay. You're not asking me to strip down, or parade around in front of some horny women."

"Well, all of my friends are pretty horny. Just not for you."

"True. I mean it, though. I can do this. I *want* to do this."

She gives me one of the smiles that are mine alone. "Meet me at my car in five minutes, okay?"

"You want to go out?" I ask. It's Sunday, and we're both in t-shirts. I have on ratty jeans, and she's wearing yoga pants.

"Trust me, Soldier."

"Always, Angel. Always."

* * *

Jade

I know what I need to do. I grab the envelope from our apartment, and rush back downstairs. Nate is waiting by my car. After opening my door for me, he slides into the passenger seat, and I drive.

"No, Jade," he says when he sees where I'm going.

"Yes."

"You deserve more than this."

"I only care about marrying you. I don't need the big wedding. I just need you."

I pull into the driveway of the drive-thru wedding chapel, and he grabs my arm. "We don't have the marriage license."

"What do you think I needed the five minutes for? I obviously didn't change."

"You're sure about this? I meant it when I said I was okay with the wedding."

"I'm sure. My dad may want to kill us, but he'll understand. So will the girls."

"Thank you. I'll make this up to you somehow."

"There's nothing to make up. We're getting married. That's all that matters to me. I shouldn't have let things get so out of control. I just…I got caught up in all of it."

"We could've changed, you know. I would've put on my tux, and you could've worn your pretty dress."

"How do you know it's pretty?"

"You'd be in it. How could it not be pretty?"

"I think I'm swooning in this car."

"Seriously, though. Do you want to go back and change first?"

"No," I tell him honestly. "We're not fancy dresses and tuxes. This is us, jeans and yoga pants. I won't deny that I was looking forward to being a girl for a day, but I like that we can just be us."

Nate looks me up and down. "Angel, you are always a girl. And I fucking love every inch of you."

"I love your inches, too. Now let's get married so I can take you home and play with him."

"He's very happy that you're thinking about him right now."

"He always is."

"True."

He grabs my hand and kisses it as I put the car into gear and drive up to the window. I hand over our license, and Nate's credit card, because he insisted on paying. Less than five minutes later we've said "I do," placed the rings I grabbed on each other's fingers, and kissed as man and wife. I can honestly say I've never been happier in my life. I don't need a dress, or a cake, especially now that I know Nate would've been uncomfortable. I have him, and that's everything I need.

* * *

Nate

I wake up to Jade's tongue moving across my spine. I know she's licking the tribal tattoo I have running down my back, and it feels damn good. "Morning, Angel."

"You know what today is?"

"Our wedding day."

"Until I kidnapped you."

"Best day of my life."

It was. Even though her dad and all of her friends flipped out. Once Jade told them why we did it, they admitted it was the best thing for us. I still hate that she gave up her fancy wedding, which is why I worked with Stella on a surprise for today.

"Mine too. We should just stay in bed today. You know, start our honeymoon early."

"We've been on a honeymoon since you came to Paris and brought me home."

"True, but tomorrow it's official. Two weeks on a private island. Just you and me."

"And my cock. You know how sad he gets when you forget him."

"I'll never forget him."

"To get back to your original statement, we can't stay in bed today."

"Why not?"

"We have a reception to get ready for."

"A reception? What did you do, Soldier?"

"I didn't *do* anything. I just didn't *undo* anything, either."

She sits up and stares at me in shock. "You didn't call anyone to cancel?"

"The ceremony, yes. Just not the reception."

"Nate."

"Jade."

"I can't let you do this."

"It's already done."

"I didn't expect this."

"You weren't supposed to."

"You're really okay with this?"

My heart swells as I see the worry in her eyes. "Yes, Angel. I want to see you in your pretty dress, I want to smash wedding cake in your face, and I want to dance with you all night."

"Swooning again."

"Good."

"Can I ask for one thing?"

"You can ask for a million things."

"I just want one. Can you just wear your vest, and not your jacket? No tie, and your sleeves rolled up?"

"You want some stubble too, don't you?"

"Yes. Please," she moans.

"Done."

She grabs my cock, but I reluctantly pull her hand off of me.

"He wants me."

"24/7. No doubt. I want you too, but Stella will be here any minute."

"She'll understand. She's the last person who'd cock-block me."

"Behave, Mrs. Anderson."

"Never, Mr. Anderson. And you know damn well that you love it when I misbehave."

I smile and pull her close. "I do. Later. You can do whatever you want to me later."

"I'm going to hold you to that."

"Please do."

She leans over me, and I know she's not going to wait. The doorbell rings before she can make me push her away again. Which is a good thing, because honestly I don't know if I *could* push her away a second time. Saved by the bell.

* * *

Jade

"You cock-blocked me, Stell," I tell her when I open the door.

She looks horrified. "Go back upstairs! I'll come back, or just come to my place. What do you need? Five minutes? Ten?"

"She *needs* to go get ready. And five minutes, Stell? I didn't know you had such a low opinion of me," Nate tells her.

"You can't get her off in five?" she asks him with a smirk.

"Oh, he can, believe me he can," I say with a laugh.

"Then it isn't an insult, is it? Besides, you know I love you, Nate. Especially since I didn't have to cancel the party."

"Love you too, Stell. Now get out."

"Nate!"

"He just wants us to go get ready so he can see you in your dress."

"Very true."

He kisses me hard and then pushes me out the door as Stella laughs. "Have fun with your hand," she tells him as he flips her off before closing the door.

We take the elevator to her floor, and when the doors open, all of my girls are there. They're in robes with champagne glasses in their hands. Ellie hands me one and pulls me into a hug. We hold onto each other for a full minute, while everyone else lets us have our space. She understands why I did what I did, but I know it hurts her.

"I'm sorry," I tell her again.

"Don't ever be sorry for making Nate comfortable. I just wish I could've seen it."

"You've seen the video."

"I know. And I'm sorry I've been kind of a bitch about it."

"You haven't. If you were being a bitch, you'd be telling me I can't still be your matron of honor."

"That would never happen. I love you, J."

"I love you too, El."

"Are you two done now? We all still have hair and makeup to take care of," Stella reminds us.

"Yes, boss," Ellie tells her.

We spend the next few hours getting ready. I love these women so much, and I also respect the hell out of them. I'm so glad I get the chance to wear my dress and have them with me. The wedding wasn't important, but having my friends with me to celebrate is. I never told Nate, because I didn't want him to feel any pressure at all to do what I wanted, but I was a little sad.

Stella has me step into my dress, and I smile into the mirror once it's on. The dress has an embroidered, strapless, sweetheart neckline. The front is a few short, ruffled layers of soft material, but the back is long enough to trail behind me on the floor. There are a couple of big pink flowers at my waist, too. Pink isn't really my color, but I really love them. To top things off, Stella found me a poufy hat thing to wear on the side of the updo she did for me.

Sparkly shoes with flowers and pearls crossing over each other complete what was to be my wedding look. I feel totally girly, and I love it.

The rest of the girls are in brown strapless dresses that have beading over the top and side. They all look gorgeous, especially Audrey with her baby bump. She still has about three months, and none of us can wait. Tegan's pregnant too, but she's barely showing. I think about having a baby with Nate, and I'm surprised to find that I want one. I never planned to have kids, but I want to have Nate's baby. I'm not sure he's ready for that, but I need to talk to him about it. Later. Right now, I have something else I need to do.

"I'll meet you all in the tent, okay?"

"You're going to see that horse, aren't you?" Stella asks me with a laugh.

"Yes. I want to see my boy before I go out to my man."

"I knew you would. Here, put these shoes on," she says, handing me some plain grey sandals. "And please try not to totally ruin your dress in the barn."

"I'll try."

I really do try. I hold the back of my dress up until I get to Cherub's stall. I let it go to hug and kiss him, but I don't move too much so I hope it's okay. If not, I'll deal with Stella's wrath. I just need to see him.

"How did I know you'd be here?" Nate asks from behind me.

"I just wanted to see him for a minute."

"I know. I'm not jealous of him anymore. Much."

I turn to my husband. "You have nothing to be jealous about, and you know it. Cherub is like our kid, just in horse form."

"We never talk about kids."

"I wasn't sure you wanted them," I say, biting my lip.

"Do you?"

"Yeah. I want a little Nate."

"Well, I want a little Jade."

"We may have to wait a couple of months. You know, because of the super birth control, and also because some of us still need to do missions for a few more months at least."

"We have forever, Angel."

"Yes we do, Soldier."

He picks me up into his arms and carries me out to the office area of the stable where I left my pretty shoes. I switch them out once he sets them down, and then we walk hand in hand to the reception tent. All of the boxing-themed things I picked with Stella look amazing. Nate and I both love the boxing ring centerpieces that are filled with roses, and feature different famous boxers. Our cake with the fighting couple is great, too. And honestly, even if this whole place was in shambles, it would be perfect. I'm married to Nate, and we both want kids. What more could a girl want?

DARCY & BRAYDEN

<u>Brayden</u>

I look over at Darcy sleeping next to me, and cringe. Not because I would want her anywhere else, but because she's forced to be here with me in the castle. We're getting ready for our royal wedding, and I know she hates it. She hates every minute she's had to spend taking formal pictures and being interviewed for magazines. I thank God every day that she loves me enough to put up with this shit. I don't know what I'd do if she told me it was too much for her.

"What's wrong, Bray?" she asks in a sleepy voice.

"Just thinking. Go back to sleep, Cat."

"Stop worrying about the weddings. I'm fine. We get to have our real wedding first, and I can pretend to be a princess for a day after that."

"You hate it."

"But I love you. I would marry you 100 times if that's what we needed to do. It's really not a big deal."

"I love you so much. You know that right?"

"I think I got the memo when you gave up your kingdom for me," she tells me with a smirk.

"I'd give up 100 kingdoms for you."

"We're getting too sappy this early in the morning. Go back to sleep with me, Crown."

"You'll have a crown in a few days, you know."

"I still can't believe you let me have so many diamonds for it."

"You could have them all if you wanted them. Plus, you picked the citrine for your ring," I remind her, holding up her hand to look at the large orange stone surrounded by small diamonds on the gold band.

"I wanted color."

"I'm well aware of your love for the color orange," I tell her as I slide my hand through her hair.

She sits up suddenly and looks serious. "Is it okay that I had my ring made out of a lesser gem? You've never said anything, but did Parliament give you trouble?"

They did, but I didn't want to tell her. "They would've preferred a diamond, or even a sapphire, but it's not their ring." Which is exactly what my Uncle Steven told them.

"Does the crown make up for it a little?"

"Yes. I need you not to worry about it, though. Parliament can go fuck themselves for all I care."

"If I can't worry about Parliament, then you can't worry about me having to endure a royal wedding."

"I'm going to make things as easy for you as possible. I promise."

"I don't need easy, Bray. You should know that by now. Nothing in my life has ever been easy."

"Including me."

"You," she says with a mischievous smile. "You are wonderfully hard."

"Why yes I am."

I roll over on top of her and show her just how hard I am. A couple of hours later, we both fall into a sound sleep, sated and happy. I think of all she's been through as I drift off, and I vow to keep my promise and make the weddings easy for her. It's the least I can do.

* * *

Darcy

"Get off the bloody railing before you fall," Jenysis tells me.

"I won't fall," I reply.

"Stella will kill you if you ruin your wedding dress."

"Spoilsport," I tell her, knowing she's right.

Today is my *real* wedding to Brayden. The one that's just for us and our friends and family. It will be informal and fun, just like we are in our daily lives. My man may be a prince, but he has adapted to a "normal" life with me in Las Vegas rather easily.

For today, I get to wear a whimsical dress. It's strapless with some embroidery on top. The bottom has asymmetrical satin and chiffon ruffles before falling into just layers of chiffon on the bottom. I love it, and I love the bridesmaids dresses my friends are all wearing.

They're orange with one strap of flowers and some embroidery on top. The bottom skirt barely comes to the top of their thighs, but there's long pieces of chiffon crisscrossing to the floor. It's something I would wear, and I'm glad they love them as well. Especially since they can't all stand with me at the other wedding. There it will just be Jen and some of her distant royal cousins.

Even though I'm excited for today, I couldn't resist taking a walk on the balcony railing. It overlooks the sea, and was just too inviting for me to ignore. I didn't think anyone would miss me, but obviously they did. Or at least Jen did. I was hoping to talk to her alone anyway.

"How are you doing?" I ask.

"I'm brilliant. Joining the Society is a dream come true for me. I can't wait for training to begin."

"I'm glad about that, but I was referring to you and Wayne."

Society Weddings • 107

"That's not a thing. *We're* not a thing."

"Why not?"

"Because he's a stupid arse who just wants to bang as many birds as possible."

"Whoa. You're really mad at him. I knew you were upset, but you've gone all common with your language there, Princess."

"Oh bugger off, Darcy."

"I didn't mean to upset you," I tell her as tears start to form in her eyes.

"I think I love him. I'm just a daft cow for thinking he was interested in more than just shagging me."

"No, you're not. He's into you. Like seriously into you. You two just need to talk."

"I'm scared to talk to him."

"Society girls are not scared of talking to men."

"Oh really? Because I don't think any of you had a smooth road to romance."

"Touché. I still think you should talk to him, but you do what you need to do."

"Right now, I need to get you to the chapel."

"Lead the way," I tell her, sliding my heels back on.

We walk to the small chapel on the castle grounds. There's not much space in there, but we don't need it. Most of our friends are in the wedding, so only the mentors and a few other people need to sit. We're keeping things short and sweet with our own vows, and then the kiss.

"Looking good, sis," Noah tells me when we walk up.

He looks great in his black suit and orange tie. "You too, little brother."

We hug each other tight, and I take his arm as everyone lines up in front of us. For this wedding, my brother will be walking me down the aisle. Taking a cue from Faith, we have reserved seats up front for both my dad and Brayden's. Mallory is in the front row on my side with my mother. She didn't recognize me today, but it means everything to me that she's here.

I see Brayden as soon as I clear the chapel door. His eyes light up when he sees me, and I know I'm grinning like a fool. I see him in suits almost every day, but it never gets old. He's sexy as sin and I can't wait to make love to him for the first time as his wife. His smile turns into a smirk, and I know he sees the desire on my face. Since there are no cameras in here, except for the ones we hired, I stick out my tongue at him as everyone laughs.

After shaking hands with Noah, Brayden takes my hand and leans in close. "You look beautiful, Cat."

"Thanks."

The official we hired says and does all of the normal wedding things, and then it's time for our vows. I smile at Brayden as we turn towards each other and he begins.

"I once tried to make a list of things to do so I could impress you. Everyone here knows that didn't go so well. I decided that instead of trying to impress you with promises today, I'm just going to be honest, so here goes.

"I promise to never play video games with you when you're online with your gamer friends, because we both know I'll get you killed no matter how hard I try not to. I promise to dress up as whatever character you want and go to those nerd conventions you love. I swear to never try and ride a bronco, cook for you, or sing in drag again. I will, however, order in your favorite foods, give you foot massages, and make love to you every night. You've shown me what true love and loyalty really are, and I promise to love you forever, my Cat."

Tears are running down my face, and he reaches up to kiss them away. "I promise to never break into your vault again, to never make you think you need to impress me, and to never make you dress up as anything too crazy when you go to the conventions with me. I'll cook for you when I'm not too tired from work, play the part of the perfect princess when you need me to, and make love to you every morning when we wake up. I never thought I'd find love, and I swear that no matter what happens, I'm never going to stop loving you or doing everything I can to make you happy. I love you, my Crown."

"I don't know what to even say after those vows, so yeah Brayden, just go ahead and kiss your bride," the officiant tells us.

We kiss and then hug each other before turning to our guests. Everyone is cheering as we lead them to one of the smaller ballrooms in the castle. I can't wait for this part—Brayden wanted to surprise me with the reception, so I have no clue what to expect.

I stop inside the door and practically tackle my husband when I see what he's done. "You should probably see everything before you take me to the ground," he tells me with a laugh.

There are gaming stations everywhere with big screen TVs, and each table is themed for a different game I love. The cake topper is a groom dragging his bride from her game controllers while Call of Duty is on the TV screen. It's perfect. All of it is so very perfect for me. But what about him?

"There's nothing for you here, Bray?"

"You're here, and you're my wife. That's honestly all I'll ever need."

"I didn't need all of this, either. I seriously love it, but I would've been okay with anything."

"I know. You may not have needed it, but you deserve the reception of your dreams. It's my mission in life to make all of your dreams come true, so why not start with this?"

I kiss him hard, and start planning all the ways I'm going to thank him more properly once we're alone. I love my prince, and I'm ready for my fairytale ending.

* * *

Brayden

"Will Darcy behave today?" my mother asks, coming up next to me to wait for the carriage bringing my wife from the castle to the cathedral.

She wanted to walk, but her damn dress is too heavy, so she settled for an open carriage. I know she'll be making several stops to greet the people of my country along the road, but that's why they love her. "My wife will do whatever she damn well pleases."

"The world is watching this wedding."

"The world loves Darcy, just as our people do."

She doesn't say anything else, because she can't. Darcy has won over every heart here, except for hers and a few members of Parliament. I don't really care what anyone else thinks. I'll never ask her to be someone she isn't.

"It's time to go inside," Noah tells me. "She's almost here."

Since no one knows about our real wedding last night, we have to uphold tradition. I'm not supposed to see her until she walks down the aisle. I saw her when she reluctantly left our bed this morning, but I can't wait to see her coming down the aisle to me again. That will never get old.

I take my place next to Noah, who I insisted be here with me. The Society girls and their guys, as well as the mentors and the Griffin family, are all here again, but this time they're in the pews and not standing with us. I wish things could be different, but protocol demands things from me, and sometimes I can only push back so far.

I watch as my cousins walk up the aisle in dark orange gowns suited for princesses. Embroidered bodices and full skirts are quite a contrast to what Darcy's friends wore last night, but at least she got her color. It's something.

Jen smiles at me as she takes her place, and then everyone stands for my girl. My knees go weak when I see her coming down the long aisle on the arm of my Uncle Steven. The gown she has on is so wide that it almost touches the pews as she walks. It's got an off the shoulder neckline and is covered in beading and diamonds. It's elaborate and formal. Nothing Darcy would ever choose for herself, and now I realize why it was too heavy to walk in. The crown she designed is on top of her orange hair that has been swept up into a fancy twist. The rows of diamonds with no space in between stand out brilliantly on top of her bright hair, and I'm glad she got her way and has no veil cascading down her back. A veil would make what she's wearing too over to the top. As it is, the white roses she's carrying look bland next to her gown and crown. She looks gorgeous, and my heart hurts thinking about how she's doing all of this for me.

My uncles kisses her on the cheek before placing her hand in mine. "I'm so sorry," I whisper as we turn towards the bishop who will be presiding over this spectacle. "So very sorry."

She looks at me with concern shining in her eyes, and it makes me feel even more guilty. My gamer girl doesn't deserve what I've let my mother do to her. I didn't promise to protect her when we said our vows, because she's a certified bad-ass and can take care of herself most of the time. Not now, though. She did this for me. She's hiding who she really is for me, and it kills me to know I've taken her spirit away, even if it's only for a few minutes.

* * *

Darcy

I'm really worried about Brayden. From the moment he apologized to me in the church, he's been distant, giving me guilty looks every once in a while, but none of his smiles I love him so much. No one but me, and maybe Noah or Jen, would see it, but it's there. He's upset, and right now I can't ask him why.

We're in a dark hall at the castle. It's filled with stone arches, under which dozens of elaborate gold and white tables and chairs have been placed. This room looks nothing like our reception last night, and I'm scared that my dress won't even make it past the tables to where we are supposed to sit at the front of the room.

I continue to smile and shake hands as people come through the receiving line, but when the last person passes, I grab Brayden and start to pull him from the room. His mother tries to stop me, but I glare at her before pulling him outside. Once we're far enough from the party, I drop his hand and cross my arms over my chest.

"What did I do wrong?"

"You? You did nothing wrong, Cat," he says, finally looking at me.

"Then why didn't you look at me during the ceremony?"

"How could I look at you knowing I did this to you?" he asks, gesturing to my dress.

"It's just a dress, Crown."

"It's so dam big it probably needs its own zip code."

"Well yeah, but who cares? Again, it's just a dress."

"It's not you."

And now I get it. He thinks this stupid dress is hiding the real me. "No, it's not. But in the time you've known me, have I ever let my clothes define who I am?"

"Definitely not."

"Then why would you think this dress would? I'm still the same beer drinking chick you fell for. I can dress up, but nothing will change who I am. Does it suck to have to pretend to be formal? Yeah, it does. And if this was our real wedding, I'd be a little upset. It's just for show today, though, so I really don't care. We'll pretend for a few more hours, and then I'll take off this dress, let my hair down, and let you fuck me until we both pass out."

"I hate to interrupt, but people are noticing that you're gone," Nate says, walking outside with a smirk on his face.

"And they sent you?" I ask, putting a hand on my hip.

"Why not? You are one of my best friends."

"You mean they were afraid we were doing more than talking and figured you wouldn't be shocked."

"Well, I did walk in on the two of you in the game room last week. I still don't understand how you got into that position on the foosball table," he says shaking his head, and then fist bumping Brayden.

"I have skills," my husband tells him.

"Yes, you do, but we aren't talking about them with Nate. Now or ever."

"What if we've already talked? I know you and the girls talk."

"Just get inside. Both of you."

I start to walk in front of them, but Brayden spins me and pulls me into his arms for a hard kiss. I kiss him back as Nate chuckles. For a cat burglar who never thought she'd find friendship or love growing up, I'm happy to say I've found both. I have great friends, and a husband who fits together with me like he's my missing piece. Happily ever after isn't just for fairytales.

ELLIE & AIDEN

<u>Ellie</u>

"I have to admit that I never thought we'd be having a traditional wedding in a church. Or a backyard reception," Aiden tells me, looking at the overflowing book I have on our dining room table.

"You don't mind, do you?" I ask, getting a little scared.

"Nah, whatever you want is fine with me, Doll."

"Good. You had me worried there for a minute."

"There is one thing, though. I was hoping I could do something out of the ordinary for you."

"How out of the ordinary?"

"Um, I guess a lot?"

My heart starts to beat fast. I love Aiden, but I've always dreamed of what my wedding would be like. I compromised a little on the bridesmaid dresses, because Stella found some cool ones that look like waves and Aiden did propose on the beach. I guess I could compromise a little more. Just a little.

"What did you have in mind?"

"I can't tell you. I want it to be a surprise."

"Then how am I supposed to agree or not agree? You can't just spring things on me a week before our wedding!" I yell. I'm aggravated, and why not? He hasn't planned this wedding. I haven't let him, but still.

"Maybe you could trust me. Novel concept, I'm sure, but it would be damn nice for once."

"What are you even talking about? You know I trust you."

"Really? So that's why I couldn't do the cake tasting on my own when you couldn't fly to Chicago?"

"My mom wanted to be part of it."

"It had nothing to do with the fact that you said I wouldn't know buttercream from cream cheese frosting if one of them bit me? Or that you knew I'd choose chocolate and vanilla because I have simple tastes? Your mom had her volume turned up and I heard you, El."

"Aiden, I…I'm sorry. I just want this wedding to be like I dreamed it would be. I thought you wanted that, too."

"Don't. Don't you dare try and guilt me into thinking I might be wrong. You're a fucking bridezilla, and I'm done. Just done."

"What do you mean you're done? Where are you going?" I ask as he grabs his jacket and heads for the door.

"I'm going to hang out with my dad. Text me where and when to show up and I'll be there, but I can't be around you while you get crazier and crazier."

"That's not fair. I just want us to be happy at our wedding."

"No. You want *you* to be happy at our wedding. You don't give a fuck about what I want, or don't want. Hell, I can't even plan a surprise for you."

"Aiden, please."

"I have to go before I call off this whole thing. I'll text you when I land."

He walks out without even kissing me goodbye. He's never done that before. Am I really being crazy? I thought I was just acting like a normal bride. My girls will tell me the truth. I page them all to our apartment, thinking they'll agree that Aiden's overreacting, but when has anything ever gone the way I thought it would?

"You've been acting like a total bitch," Jade tells me. "You know I love you, but I don't blame Aiden for leaving."

"I just want my wedding to be perfect."

"We know. You tell us at least five times a day," Ainsley says.

"All of you had the weddings of your dreams, so why can't I?"

"You can honey, but you have to calm down about some things. You do know that the marriage is more important than the wedding, right?" Tegan asks me.

"Yeah." I do. Really I do.

"What set him off?" Stella asks.

"He said he wanted to surprise me with something that wasn't traditional. I freaked out a little."

"Like you did when I wanted to shave one side of my hair?" Darcy asks.

"Or was it like when you realized your brother has a basketball game the night before, and can't fly in until the morning of the wedding?" Isa asks.

"When you put it that way, I do sound like a bitch. God, what am I going to do? I didn't mean to go crazy."

"Well first, you need to tell him you want your surprise," Stella says looking down at her phone. "He just texted me to cancel it, and believe me, you want it."

"I do want it. I want anything he wants to give me. I'm such an idiot."

"Nah. You're just a crazy bridezilla," Faith tells me. "I went a little crazy, too."

"Not like me. I need to chill out. I used to be the most chill person I knew, and now I've become this…this psycho."

"We're all here for you, El. We'll keep you in line," Reina tells me with a smile.

"Thanks. Now if you'll excuse me, I have a fiancé to call."

"Give him some good phone sex," Audrey advises with a smirk as they all file out.

I just smile back. If that's what it takes, I'm more than happy to play a little. Or a lot.

* * *

Aiden

I'm staring out the window, contemplating how my amazing fiancé has turned into a crazy person, when my phone rings. Ainsley has all the jets set up with satellite cell capabilities, but I was hoping for a quiet flight. I look down and see that it's Ellie. My finger hovers over accept, but I ended up tapping decline. I just can't talk to her yet. I wait, but there's no voicemail. I'm glad. I don't want recorded messages from her. I just want her.

Which means I should just go along with what she wants, but then again, I've never been that guy. The one who just goes along with everything, and never speaks his mind. I'm not wired that way. She's wrong in this situation, and maybe leaving town wasn't exactly right, but I was hanging so far off the ledge that I seriously considered canceling the whole thing. Deep down I know that's not what I want, which is why I borrowed a jet.

I love Ellie more than anything, but I had to get away. Now that she's called, I keep looking at my phone, wondering if she'll try again. When fifteen minutes pass, and she hasn't, I bite the proverbial bullet, and initiate a call of my own. It rings so many times that I think she won't answer, but then she does.

"I'm so sorry, Hawk."

Her voice sounds so small and sad that I can feel my heart crack. "I shouldn't have left."

"I'm a crazy bridezilla."

"You're *my* crazy bridezilla."

"I'd like whatever surprise you want to give me. If you still want to give me something, I mean."

"I want to give you everything, Doll. I just need to know you want it."

"I do. And I want our cake to be chocolate with vanilla buttercream. Just the way you like it."

"What about your lemon zest or peach meringue or whatever?"

"It was red velvet," she says with a laugh.

"I like red velvet."

"Yes, but you love chocolate, so that's what we're getting."

"I don't expect you to change the wedding, or what you want, just for me. I just want to feel like I'm involved."

"That's so progressive of you. Next you'll be getting manicures."

"You're so cute. Not."

"What else do you want to do or have?"

"Nothing else, El. I just want to marry you, and give you a surprise. I appreciate the cake."

"I love you, Aiden. I'm going to try and be better."

"I love you, too. Just be yourself, and we'll be fine."

"Are you coming home?"

"No. I still think I should see my dad for a couple of days, but then I'll fly to Chicago and meet you there, okay?"

"Sounds perfect. Tell your dad hi for me. I'll miss you."

"I'll miss you too. Can I call you when I get settled?"

"Please do. I was told I needed to partake in some epic phone sex with you."

"Audrey?"

"Yes."

"Blake is one lucky man. This pregnancy seems to have made her super horny."

"Can you imagine what would happen if I got pregnant? I might kill us both."

I'm silent for almost a full minute, because I have imagined Ellie being pregnant with my baby. Not because we'd probably never leave our bed for nine months, but because I just want a kid with her. Despite the crazy stuff we've both been through and done, I know we'd be great parents. I don't want to scare her, but at the same time I want her to know.

"Yeah. Actually. I *can* imagine you being pregnant."

"Me too," she says softly.

"We'll talk when I get to Chicago. Okay?"

"Okay."

"Love you, Hawk."

"Love you, Doll."

* * *

<u>Ellie</u>

I'm in Chicago, and everything is going great. Now that I've calmed down about everything, it's all going better than I thought it would. Aiden and I have been talking several times a day, and he's flying in tonight. His dad will fly in on Friday, just in time for the rehearsal dinner at my parents' flagship pub.

The only issue I'm having is with my brother, Dylan. When I planned the wedding, I had no idea that he'd suddenly become an NBA star. He's been playing in the league for a couple of years, but always in the background. This season he got a chance to start, and he's been burning up the court. He's supposed to fly in early Saturday morning, but he hasn't told me what time to have the jet ready. It's time to try and call him again.

"Hello, Dylan Gallagher's phone," a woman says after two rings.

"Who is this?"

"His girlfriend."

"He doesn't have a girlfriend."

"He does now, bitch, so you can back off and forget about getting with him. In fact, forget this number."

She hung up on me. His nighttime snack just hung up on me. Oh hell no. I tap my phone to dial him again. This time it takes her four rings to answer.

"Put my brother on the phone now, *bitch*, or I swear I'll fly out there and kick your ass."

"You're his sister?"

"Yeah, and you're his one nighter who should've been gone already. So give my brother his phone, and fuck off."

"Maybe I won't. How do I know you're his sister?"

Before I can rain down some hell on her, Dylan's on the line. "El?"

"Since when did you let the one timers answer your phone?"

"I was in the shower."

"Alone? She was that bad?"

He laughs. "I don't remember, so I thought I should be safe rather than sorry."

"You know you put the 'whore' in manwhore, right?"

"Tsk, tsk, little girl. You're above the name calling."

"Normally, yes. But that C U Next Tuesday pissed me off. Is she still there?"

"Not for long. Hold on." He doesn't even bother to cover the phone as he sends her on her way. "Sorry about that, sis."

"You really need to slow down. I know you're a big star now, but these hook-ups are going to get old."

"I know. I just haven't found anyone who interests me for more than a few minutes."

"You will."

"I hope so. I'm guessing you didn't call to give me love advice, so what's up?"

"It was sex advice, and I need to know what time you need the jet on Saturday."

"Oh, yeah. I can be at the airport by six. Wouldn't want to be late to my baby sister's wedding."

"Good thing you're playing in NYC."

"It is."

"I love you, Dyl Pickle. Have a good game on Friday, and I'll see you on Saturday."

"Love you too, Ellie Bear. And thanks."

I hang up and head out to the airport to pick up my own guy. He doesn't know I'm picking him up, but I need to. Phone calls are no substitute for the real thing, and I need to have him look me in the eye, and tell me we're okay, before I can totally believe him.

* * *

Aiden

"You look like you need to relax," I tell Ellie, coming up behind her and massaging her shoulders.

Tomorrow is the wedding, and while she's dialed back the crazy, I know she's still worried that everything won't go as planned. I'll be sleeping alone tonight, but there's no tradition against me making her come a few times before the rehearsal.

"What do you have in mind?"

"Whatever you want?"

"Anything?"

"You know it."

She grabs my hand and pulls me outside and into her car. We drive to her parents' house. They're working, but the grounds are overrun with event people setting up for our wedding reception that will be going on in the backyard tomorrow. She grabs my hand and sprints up the stairs. I've only been on the ground floor, so I'm shocked when she takes me to the attic, and I see that this was her room, and nothing has been changed.

There is still a twin bed with a teal and black comforter. Posters of boy bands are on the walls, and there are pictures of her family and friends around her mirror.

"El?"

"When I was a silly teenage girl, I wanted to have a boy to sneak in here and make love to me on my bed," she says as she pulls her clothes off.

"And now?"

"Now I want my sexy man to fuck me, and break the bed doing it."

"I can do that," I tell her as I undress.

"I know."

Before she knows what's happening, I grab her and flip her upside down. I've been wanting to do this again ever since we sixty-nined like this in D.C. I've been hoping she wanted it like this, too, and when she takes my cock deep into my mouth, I know she does.

I lick and nibble on her clit and pussy while she sucks me like her life depends on it. I'm going to come hard, and then I'm going to break her little bed. I feel the tingles up my spine, and walk us to the bed so I can play her with my fingers and make her come first.

I get three fingers in her and twist them just like she needs them. My orgasm is barreling down on me, and I can't hold off much longer. I press my tongue flat on her clit, and then she's going off. She rides my face as I come down her throat. I'm still semi-hard, so she keeps sucking.

While she brings me fully back to life, I bring her another explosive orgasm that has her squeezing my balls and arching her back so far I'm afraid it might break. And then it's on.

I spin her and then flip her. She's barely settled before I'm slamming into her. "Fuck, El. You're still pulsing around my cock."

"Yes."

"Do you want to come on my cock?"

"You know I do."

"You feel how hard you made me with that sinful mouth of yours? I fucking love being inside your mouth."

"Better than my pussy?"

I hold her hips and grind into her. "Nothing's better than your pussy, Doll. It's made for my cock to fuck hard and deep."

"So deep."

"You're going to be thinking about me tonight when you're alone in this broken bed, aren't you? Touching yourself and thinking about how good I can fuck you."

"The bed's not broken."

"It's about to be."

It's creaking, and I know it's close to collapsing. This bed was meant for her to sleep on, not get fucked so hard. A few more hard thrusts should do it.

"Break it for me, Hawk. Break the bed and watch how hard I come for you."

Oh yeah. That's what I needed to hear. I grab onto the metal slats for leverage while I push my feet against the ones at the bottom of the bed. It takes exactly five more thrusts and then the first bolts snap loose. Seconds later, we're bouncing onto the floor as Ellie screams my name. I growl out hers as I follow right after her.

Damn, how did I ever live without this? Without her? Even without the spectacular sex, she's perfect for me, and she's mine. All mine.

* * *

Ellie

Stella and the girls descend on my room way too early. Aiden was right when he said I'd be thinking about him while lying on my broken bed. I got myself off three times, and it wasn't enough. I'm still aching for him. What he did to me in this room was H-O-T hot. It's always explosive when we come together, but this took things to another level. One the teenage me couldn't have even imagined.

"Aiden was here?" Stella asks, gesturing to the bed.

"Yesterday afternoon," I admit with a smirk.

"Very nice, El," Jade tells me, giving me a high five.

We all laugh for a few minutes as they tease me, and then it's time to get ready. My mom comes up and shakes her head when she sees my bed again. It's not like I could hide it last night when she came to tuck me in. Yes, I'm in my twenties, but I still let my mom tuck me in. Nothing wrong with being sentimental before getting married.

The girls all put on their "wave" gowns. The dresses are sleeveless and go from black and light blue designs on top to silver designs over a sheer netting that is white underneath. They really do look like the ocean.

My dress is a strapless, sweetheart princess gown. The top has a little embroidery, and the stiff skirt folds over onto itself a few times. I have a peal trimmed, sheer shrug to wear over it in the church. I'm also going to wear a veil over my dark waves, and I'm carrying a pretty white bouquet. Or at least I think I am.

When all of the flowers are passed out, my bouquet is not with them. I'm freaking out a little until Stella hands me a white box. I open it to find a bouquet made of seashells mixed with white roses, along with a note from Aiden.

Doll,

I hope you like my surprise. If not, Stella has your other bouquet. The beach was where you gave me the greatest gift I've ever gotten—a promise of forever with you. I wanted to have something you could use for the wedding, and we could have after. No worries if you don't like it for the wedding. We can still put it in our apartment when we get home.

I love you,
Hawk aka the guy who'll be at the end of the aisle.

"You are using that one, right?" Stella asks.

"Of course I am," I tell her as I wipe tears from my eyes.

I almost missed out on this beautiful gift. And if Aiden was a lesser man, I might've lost him, too. I thank God and my friends for bringing me back to my senses. All I need to do now is marry my man.

* * *

<u>Aiden</u>

I smile at the Society girls as they walk down the aisle, but I'm bouncing on my feet as I wait for Ellie to appear. I hope she's got my bouquet, but if she doesn't, I'll do my best to hide my disappointment. We're getting married, and nothing else really matters.

Sunlight is streaming through the stained glass windows here in Ellie's church. She was baptized here, and other things I don't know much about. I just know she wanted to be married here, and that's good enough for me. The pews are decorated with clusters of white roses and candles in blue glass holders. I barely glance at all of it as I look for Ellie. It's been almost a minute since Jade made her way down the aisle, and the little Griffin girls have finished dropping their petals. It's time.

The wedding march starts, and there she is. I smile at her princess dress and traditional veil that hides her face. I never expected all this tradition from her, but she's completely embraced it, and as long as she's smiling all day and night, I don't care what we do. I'm happy to see that she bucked tradition where her bouquet is concerned, though. She's carrying the seashell bouquet I got her, and my smile grows even wider when I see it.

I step forward to meet her and her father. He lifts her veil, kisses her cheek, and places her hand in mine.

"Thanks for using my bouquet," I whisper to her.

"It's perfect. I love it, and I love you."

"I love you, too."

The ceremony goes exactly like I was told it would. I say and do everything we practiced, and when it's time, I give her the chaste kiss she asked for.

"Thank you," she tells me as everyone cheers.

"It's my pleasure. Just keep smiling for me. That's all I need today. Just to see you smiling and happy to be my wife."

She grabs my lapels and pulls my mouth back to hers. I'm shocked for a second, and then I kiss her back. There's no tongue, but we're definitely not being chaste. When we break apart, we're both smiling.

We take lots of pictures in and out of the church. We wanted Candi to enjoy herself, so we hired her friend LauraAnn to take our pictures. Once she's done, everyone piles into the limos that will take us back to the Gallagher's house. Ellie and I make out like teenagers, kissing and touching. I'm hard as a steel beam when we reach the house, and I'm glad that my suit jacket will somewhat conceal what I've got going on down below. I know Ellie's soaking wet, but she has all those dress layers on her side.

I laugh at the sign on the bar right inside the backyard, telling everyone to pick their beer. There will be champagne for the toasts, and they've got hard liquor for those who want it, but beer is the name of the game with this family. One of the many reasons I love them all.

"This is really cool," I tell Ellie, looking around.

"Thanks. I wanted to be casual, but I also wanted something different. I saw some things on Pinterest, and I ran with them."

She definitely achieved that. There are old windows with blue and grey borders hung around the borders of the yard. The tables and chairs are artfully mismatched, and ours have signs that say "Mr." and "Mrs." There are iron chandeliers, twinkle lights, and mason jars with little lights in them all over as well.

It's like nothing I've ever seen, which is perfect for us. We fell in love when we were different versions of ourselves. We've faced tragedy, pain, and some other things that no one should ever have to go through. We did it, and came out stronger, and better. The world better watch out, because Mr. and Mrs. Aiden Ford are a force to be reckoned with.

AUDREY & BLAKE

<u>Audrey</u>

"This can't be happening," I cry as Kendrick wheels me into one of the hospital rooms. "I'm getting married tomorrow."

"Sorry, Audrey, but this baby isn't going to wait."

"I didn't want to be an unwed mother."

"Then you shouldn't have had unprotected sex."

"I think I might punch you."

"Where is Blake?" he yells, stepping back.

"He said he was five minutes away. That was almost five minutes ago," one of the nurses responds.

"Thank God."

"I wasn't kidding about the punch, Kenny. These contractions are no joke."

"They aren't supposed to be. Didn't you watch the videos in the Lamaze class?"

"Um, no. That's some scary shit."

He rubs his hands over his face. "I did not sign up for this. I did not sign up for this."

"You can keep telling yourself that, but you know you love us."

"I am fond of you when you're not threatening me, yes, but love is going a little too far."

"Where is she? Where's Audrey?" I hear Blake ask as another contraction hits, and I force myself not to scream.

He's at my side, with my hand in his before it stops. I know I almost break his hand, but I can't help it. It *hurts*. I knew it would, but when you're experiencing it, you forget everything you've learned. Or at least I am currently feeling that way."

"We have to get married, Hollywood."

"We will. Stella's already calling everyone to tell them we're re-scheduling the wedding."

"I don't care about the wedding. We need to be married before this baby comes out."

"What? I don't know how I can do that, Dree."

I reach out and pull his face to within inches of mine, and pretty much growl at him. "You're a fucking movie star. Make it happen."

Another contraction descends on me, and this time I do scream. It's more out of frustration than pain, but I hear

Blake ask Kendrick how much time he has to get someone here to marry us.

"Not long. You better hurry."

* * *

Blake

I've been calling every Justice of the Peace I can find on Google, but so far no one is free to just drop everything and come here to marry us. It might have something to do with the sounds they can hear in the room behind me. Audrey is alternating between crying and screaming, and honestly, I'm about to lose my mind. When Jeanne was born, Misha didn't let me in the room because she believed I wouldn't have sex with her again if I saw our child coming out of her vagina. Audrey has no qualms about that, knowing there's pretty much nothing in the world that would keep me from having sex with her.

I'm about to give up, and just tell her it can't be done when Jeanne runs in with Wayne. "Dad. Wayne got ordained for Stella and Kace's wedding. He can marry you and Audrey."

"Seriously?" I ask the boy band singer.

"Yep. Since you were getting married tomorrow, I'm assuming you've got a license already."

"We do. It's at home."

"I'll take your word for it. Let's get this done."

"Wait for us," Reina yells, and I turn to see all of Audrey's friends running down the hall. The guys follow behind them, along with her parents.

"I'm not sure Audrey would want everyone in here," I say, planting myself in front of the door.

"Let them in. All of them. We're getting married," Audrey yells.

I turn and smile at her. "Yeah, we are."

"You're going to have to hurry," Kendrick tells us.

"I got this," Wayne tells him.

Less than two minutes later, we're legally married, and Audrey is ready to push. Everyone but Audrey's mom and Jeanne leave the room. My daughter is looking a little freaked out, which I guess is good for a teenage girl. I'm not even near ready to be a grandfather yet, so bring on the fear.

It only takes a few pushes, and then our little boy makes his appearance. He wails like he's supposed to, the nurses wrap him up, and they hand him to me. He's beautiful, and I feel myself tear up a little.

"Here he is, Dree. Our little guy, Joseph Alejandro Armstrong."

"We did it," she says, reaching out to take the baby from me and hold him close.

"*You* did it. I just held your hand."

"I love you, Blake."

"And I love you, Mrs. Armstrong."

***

<u>Audrey</u>

It's been a month since Joe was born, and I love him more every day. I don't care that he wakes me up all night, or that he already has a stubborn personality. To me, he's perfect.

My husband is pretty perfect, too. He's already planned on taking a two month break to be with me, and he does as much as he can to get me some sleep, even though I'm nursing. He watches me feed Joe with a look of wonder on his face, and no shortage of hunger in his eyes. My breasts were never small, and now they're pretty much porn star size. I don't know how much will stay once I slowly introduce formula into our routine, but I know he can't wait to get his own chance with them.

"You ready to get married again tomorrow?" Jeanne asks, practically running into the room.

"Yes," I tell her with a smile.

I'm getting my wedding tomorrow, the one we postponed when our son demanded to be born. It was important to me that we get married before he was born, because while I may be progressive with everyone else's lives, I never personally wanted to be an unwed mother, even for a day. I was okay with not having the wedding, but Blake is all about making my dreams come true, and he insisted we go ahead. Most of our guests are still able to attend, and all that I needed was a different wedding dress. I've lost most of the weight I gained, so I don't need a maternity dress anymore, and I have to admit that I love the dress Stella got me. It shows off my curves, and I know Blake is going to freak out.

"I can't wait to wear my dress. It's so pretty," Jeanne says.

"I think so, too," I tell her.

The dresses are knee-length and strapless with a sheer overlay covered in flowers. They're yellow, just like everything else in the wedding, along with my gorgeous ring. Reina hated her yellow ring, but I love mine. It has a large pear-shaped yellow diamond flanked with smaller diamonds in the same shape on the sides. Ever since we had a re-do on our prom night, and I wore a version of the yellow dress from all those years ago, yellow has been my favorite color. Stella drew the line at me wearing yellow, but she's promised me no one will miss it's meaning to me.

"I'm really happy you're my stepmom. I wish you were my real mom."

She hasn't seen Misha in months, and my heart breaks for her. "I won't ever try to come between the two of you, but I'm here for you just as much as I am for Joe. I hope you know that."

"I do, Aud. You make me feel loved every day."

"You do the same for me. I love you, Jeanne."

"Can I join in on the love fest?" Blake asks from the doorway, and I see his eyes are a little watery.

"I guess so," I tell him with a smile.

"Why don't you take a nap, Dree? Jeanne and I will take care of Joe."

"That sounds heavenly, Hollywood. Thanks."

I wait a few minutes, so my son can get his fill. When he lets go of my nipple, I see that his eyes are glazed over. I look up and Blake's are, too. I laugh as I hand Joe to Jeanne, and take my time covering back up. Who could blame me? I just had a baby, so having my husband desire me is awesome, especially since Kenny gave me the green light to have sex on my wedding night.

I climb into bed and am surprised when Blake slides in behind me. "Jeanne said I can nap with you."

"You just want to feel me up."

"Guilty. Your tits are a thing of beauty."

"And full of milk."

"I don't mind getting a little dirty. You should know that by now."

He turns me to him, and pushes my bra down to take a nipple in his mouth. He doesn't suck hard, but I think he wants to. "You can do it," I tell him.

He shakes his head and then lifts it to look at me. "I don't want your milk. It's hella sexy watching you feed our boy, but that's not a turn on for me. I just need my mouth on these."

"By all means, do what you want."

"Really? What I want?"

"Yes. Suck them to your heart's content."

"What if I want to fuck them?"

We haven't done that before, but I think I'd like that. A lot. "Oh yeah. That, too."

He nudges me so I'm flat on my back, and then pulls my bra and panties off before removing his briefs. "I want to lick your pussy while I fuck your tits."

"Yeah. That'll work."

He positions himself over me, and I squeeze my breasts tight around his cock. As he starts moving, he leans down and sucks my clit into his mouth. He begins alternating between my clit and my center and I flick my tongue out to lick his balls.

"Fuck, Dree."

"Little Hollywood likes my breasts?"

"Almost as much as your pussy."

"I can't wait for that."

He lets out a growl and starts pumping harder as we both use our tongues to drive each other crazy. He knows exactly what to do to me, exactly what I like, and it doesn't take long until he has me coming. I bite his ass to muffle my scream, and feel his thrusts grow erratic. Seconds later, his release is warm on my stomach, and he's rolling off me. I reach down and run my fingers through his cum before licking them clean.

"You're trying to kill me."

"Nah. Drive you crazy maybe, but I need you alive so we can keep doing things like that."

"Any time you want, Dree. Any fucking time. Little Hollywood and I are more than happy to oblige."

* * *

<u>Blake</u>

I walk around the grounds of the Griffin compound and marvel at what Stella's put together for us. I know Audrey picked it all, but her friend made it happen. She has to be tired after executing all these weddings, but you wouldn't know it from how she's smiling right now.

"Pretty awesome, huh?" she asks, gesturing to a set of steps that have flowers and candles all over them.

Yellow daisies spell out "LOVE" and then white and yellow flowers are all around. I also passed a cool candy and dessert bar that even has a small cake on it. Our larger cake is inside the giant tent that's been erected, and when I peeked in, I saw the elegant yellow, white, and black decorations in there. Trust my wife to make the wedding fun outside, and formal inside.

"Yeah, it is," I say as Reina approaches, rubbing her arms.

"You are not allergic to yellow," Stella tells her, rolling her eyes.

"I think I am. I'm not scratching, but seeing it everywhere is making me itch."

"You both look beautiful in your dresses," I say, trying hard not to laugh.

"They are pretty," Reina concedes. "But I'm still itchy."

"Come on, drama queen, let's get you a drink before we line up," Stella offers, shaking her head with a smile.

I wave goodbye and walk over to my place in front of the chairs. We don't have an arch or anything, because Audrey liked the idea of us being in the open in front of everyone. The white aisle is lined with square boxes filled with lemon slices, and flowers, topped by glasses filled with small white candles. It seems ridiculous, but it's actually pretty cool.

My best friend, Jesse, and I catch up while we wait. He was in the air when Audrey went into labor, so he missed the hospital ceremony. He stayed on for a few days, but he's been back at work in San Diego, which used to be my main base of operations for my movie career. Until I got a chance with Audrey, and moved to Vegas. He doesn't want to move here, and we can work separately for the most part. I really do miss him. though.

The music starts, and we both turn to watch the bridesmaids come down the aisle. Jeanne is last, holding Joe in her arms. She walks over, and I kiss them both before she hands Joe off to Audrey's mom. And then my wife is coming down the aisle on her father's arm, and all the breath leaves my body.

She's got on a full veil, but I can still make out most of her dress beneath it. It's strapless, dipping down into a scandalous "V" that has her tits pushed together, and wanting to burst free. There's some kind of flower decorations at her waist, and she's got a big, full skirt at the bottom. It looks like layers and layers of tulle. Buried treasure has always been my favorite kind, so I can't wait to go exploring.

I don't even remember her veil being lifted, or taking her hand in mine, but here she is in front of me. The woman of my dreams. She's already my wife, but that doesn't make this any less special.

"I love you, Dree."

"I love you too, Hollywood."

REINA & MATT

<u>Matt</u>

"Why are we in London, Matt?"

"This is where I got you back, so it's the perfect place to bring you to relax. You've been working hard on getting the Society academy set up, and before the recruits start in the next few months and you get too busy for me, I wanted some alone time."

"We could've relaxed closer to home, especially since I only have three days I can take off right now."

"I wanted us to have our engagement party here."

"Engagement party? We had one of those before we got married."

"Did you have fun?"

"No. But an engagement party suggests that we're having a wedding."

"We are. In two weeks."

"Here in London?"

"Nope. Mexico."

"I-I'm not ready for that, Matt."

"Which is why we're having the ceremony in the courtyard of the convent, and not the chapel. When you're ready for a church, we'll do that, too. I just want you to have something you'll love."

"I already have you."

"You know what I mean."

"Who's all going to be at this engagement party?"

"Our friends, our families, the Griffins, Aqeelah, Nev and Sully. You know, the usual."

"We could've done this in Vegas."

"Yes, but you told me that when you were here, you wished I could've been walking around with you. We'll get to Paris later, but I wanted to give you your wish here at least."

"If the people you do business knew you were such a softy, C&C would be in serious trouble."

"Good thing you're the only one who can make me soft."

"I thought I made you hard," she tells me, cupping me through my pants.

"Later," I tell her, pulling away with a smile. "We have to get changed and meet everyone at Jessica's place."

***

<u>Reina</u>

The cobalt blue dress Matt picked for me is gorgeous. I know it was him, and not Stella, because other than shoes, there aren't other accessories. I slide it on, zip it up, and twist back and forth in the mirror. The top is strapless, and the bottom falls in waves of chiffon to the floor. It's perfect.

"You ready, Rei?" Matt asks from the other side of the door. He insisted we get dressed separately so we could surprise each other.

"I am," I say, opening the door.

"Your flowers, my lady," he says, handing me a crystal encrusted clutch with a rose in the middle. "All of your necessary stuff is in there."

"It's beautiful. So is the dress. Thank you."

"Hold that thought. I have one more thing," he tells me, pulling my cuff from Tiffany out from behind his back. "I'm going to have to buy you a low cut dress so you can finally wear your necklace."

"I've worn my necklace," I remind him, pulling him down for a kiss. "Did you forget?"

"I meant in public, and no, I'll never forget coming home to find you in only that necklace, bracelet, and wedding ring."

"Good. My work here is done."

"We haven't even started, Rei."

"No, Matteo, we haven't."

"We have to go," he growls in my ear. "Stop calling me that, or I'll be forced to fuck you right here in the hall."

"What's wrong with that idea?"

"We have a party to go to."

"Fine, but when we get back, I expect an all-nighter."

"You better."

He grabs my hand and pulls me out the door. The drive to Jessica's flat from ours is short, and we're inside before I know it. I hug my parents first, thanking them for coming all this way.

"We are so happy to see *you* happy, Reina," my mother tells me.

"I really am."

"He told you about the wedding at the convent?" my father asks.

"Yes. On the grounds."

"You are still struggling with your faith?" my mother wants to know.

"I am," I admit. "I know it's there, but it's still just outside of my grasp."

"So we will have a third wedding? Maybe that was your idea all along," my father teases me.

"Yes, and no. I didn't even know Matt planned this wedding for me."

"I didn't," my husband says, kissing me on the shoulder. "I got Mother's approval, invited everyone, and maybe planned a surprise, but the other details are all up to you."

"In two weeks?"

"You *are* the head of the Society, with unlimited resources at your fingertips, aren't you?"

"Yes, but still. I have so much to do right now."

"I'll help wherever you need me, but I want this to be the wedding of your dreams."

"I'm going to take you up on that help."

"I'll help, too," my mother says, and I know she's thinking about how she missed out last time, because I didn't care about any of it.

"I'd like that."

"Can you excuse us for a moment? I have something else to show Reina," Matt says.

"Of course."

We hug my parents again, and Matt walks me over to the main dinner table. It's in front of the window and has various chandeliers over it. They range from elaborate to just circular strands of light. I love them all.

"This is so pretty. Jessica must have some awesome parties at this table."

"Maybe, but I think the chandeliers kind of make it awesome."

"They totally do. I might have to ask her where she got them."

"She borrowed them from me. Or rather, I asked her to put them up for the night."

"What?"

"These are ours. I saw something like this online, and knew you'd love them."

"I do," I tell him honestly. "We don't host many formal dinners, though."

"No, but I was thinking more about laying you out under them and licking every inch of your body."

"Do you think everyone would leave right now, including Jessica?"

"Knowing this crowd, probably."

"We can't ask them to, can we?"

"We could, but they flew all this way to celebrate with us, so we shouldn't."

"I know. A girl can dream, though, right?"

"Definitely. And then a guy can do everything in his power to make all of her dreams come true."

"You do that every day," I tell him, kissing him with every bit of feeling I have inside of me.

* * *

Matt

I look around at the community center Reina and I had built, marveling at its transformation into a full blown fiesta. Reina wanted a traditional party the whole village

Society Weddings • 151

could be invited to, and what my wife wants is what she gets. Colorful flags, along with both paper and real flowers, are everywhere. Our first wedding was all sophistication, but this one is all Reina. It's the girl who grew up here, and the woman who's never forgotten her roots.

The tables spill out of the open-air room, and into the street, where the stage is set up. There is a large area for dancing, and the smell of delicious food assaults me as I walk outside. Every woman in the village, along with some men, are cooking for us, and I can't wait to eat. After I marry my wife again, that is.

I make my way down the street, shaking hands and smiling at everyone along the way. Contrary to the bright colors surrounding me, I'm in a tan suit with a white shirt underneath. No tie, just like Reina asked of me. I would've worn a monkey suit if she wanted, and yeah, I know, I'm whipped. After all I've put her through over the years, I'm damn lucky to still have her in my life. I finally know I'm worthy of her, but that doesn't mean I'll ever take her for granted again. I won't.

I walk into the courtyard of the convent and see the chairs all set up, facing one of the fountains. There will be no officiant for our ceremony, since we're already married. No priest to bless us, because Reina isn't ready for that yet. Instead, we've chosen to do something special, something that's important to both of us.

"Hola, Matteo," Mother says, coming out to greet me.

"Hola," I reply. "Thank you again for this."

"It is my pleasure. And thank you for all you've done for this village. It has only been a few short months, and yet it is like a new place, full of life."

"This is where Reina came from. Neither of us will ever forget that."

"You are a good man."

"I'm trying to be."

"You are."

"That means a lot coming from you. Thank you."

"You're very welcome. It looks like your friends have arrived," she says, nodding to my guys who are walking outside. "I will go check on Reina."

She nods as she passes Aiden, Nate, Jake, and Theo on her way inside. "Hey guys. Glad you could make it."

"We're early, ass—oh shit, is it okay to cuss on holy ground?" Nate asks.

"You just did it, and you haven't been struck down yet," Aiden tells him.

"Try not to," I tell them all.

"Anyway, as I was saying, we're early."

"I know. I just can't resist messing with you."

"Why am I not surprised by your juvenile behavior?" Kendrick says, joining us. We've taken him out a few times, and while I'd love to say we've loosened him up, he's still a work in progress.

"Aww, Kenny, you know you love me just the way I am."

"If you say so."

"I do."

"Save that for later," Jake tells me with a smirk.

"Been there, said that, going for something new this time."

"Maybe you'll impress Reina enough for a trophy," Aiden offers.

"That's really getting old, man." Theo tells him.

"Just because they haven't won one, and you aren't even in the running, is no reason to sound bitter."

"I feel offended that I wasn't even included in that insult," Kenny tells him.

"There you go. Don't take any crap from him, Doc."

"When have I ever taken any crap from any of you?"

"True that," Nate says, holding his hand out for a fist bump.

We laugh and joke as the other Society husbands join us along with the Griffins. When Aqeelah and Neveah walk in, I excuse myself to greet them. "Hello, friends."

"Hello, Matt. Are you going to show us to our seats?" Aqeelah asks me.

"Sit wherever you'd like. There are no 'sides' here. Everyone here means something special to both of us."

"I like that," Nev says.

"I'm glad you approve. It looks like it's time for me to take my place, so we'll catch up more later, okay?"

"Of course," Aqeelah tells me, pulling me down so she can kiss my cheek. "Thank you for including us today."

"You are my family, and I want you with me always."

* * *

Reina

My wedding dress is fairly simple, and just what I wanted. The strapless bodice has a little embroidery, but not much. A little more flows onto the top layer of chiffon in the full skirt, but there is nothing sleek or flashy about this gown. My long veil is trimmed with lace, and my hair is a combination of both up and down. I feel more "me" than I ever did at my other wedding.

I smile at the girls as they finish getting ready. Stella assumed I'd want them all in my favorite color, but instead I asked for them all to wear the same dress, but in *their* favorite color. It's strapless, and the bottom looks like a flower. The rainbow is represented here today, and I love it. My culture is full of color, and I want my wedding to reflect that.

Everyone but me has a white bouquet to offset the colors of their dresses. Mine is blue roses with white and blue Calla lilies. I don't know where Stella found them, and honestly they're probably dyed, but I love them.

Society Weddings • 155

We all walk out together, and I take my father's arm as we wait for our cue. The girls all walk down the aisle, and take their seats next to their husbands. It will be only Matt and I at the fountain in front, expressing our love for each other, and everyone here with us, too.

My eyes lock with his as I make my way to where he's waiting for me. I know he's smiling, and so am I. We've come so far—past the fighting, and the hurting—and I can't wait to see where we go from here.

Matt takes my hand, and we turn to our guests. I know what he's going to say, but I'm surprised when he says it in Spanish.

"Thank you all for coming here today. You all know we're already married. This ceremony is for us, but also for you as well. Everyone in this courtyard has touched our lives, and it's our honor to recognize that now."

He squeezes my hand, as he winks at me. He's going to keep speaking in Spanish, but I'm going to switch to English. Everyone here knows some Spanish, but if he's going to honor my heritage, I'm going to honor his as well.

"Nate and Aiden, I want to thank you for always being there for Matt no matter what. Your friendship and loyalty have meant so much to him over the years, and I'm proud to consider you my friends as well."

"Audrey, thank you for listening when Reina's mother told you she had been kidnapped on her way here, and thank you for kicking my butt when I got too far out of line. You're like the big sister I never had—especially because your mom loves me so much—and we wouldn't be here right now if it wasn't for you," Matt tells her.

It's my turn again. "Thank you, Jessica, for being the parent Matt could always count on, and for loving him as much as you love Miles. Miles, thank you for coming to Las Vegas, and helping us when we needed you. I'm so honored to be part of your family, and your life."

"Mama, and Papa, thank you for giving me the gift of your daughter. I know I haven't always earned your trust, or even your respect, but when you heard we were getting married, you accepted me once again. I will spend the rest of my life proving to you that your daughter is the love of my life, and I will never hurt her again."

We continue to thank each other's friends and family, and then we come to the person we both owe so much to. Matt nods at me, telling me to go first.

"Jane, I need to thank you. For starting the Society, for rescuing me from physical danger more than once, and for trusting me to lead in your stay. I'm also so grateful for your friendship, love, and advice throughout the years. We've had a rough year, but I know in my heart that you felt you were doing the right thing."

"Gram, I owe you everything. You were there for me all my life, supporting me even when I didn't deserve it. You brought Reina to me; although, I'm pretty sure you regretted that quite often over the past decade or so. You are a strong leader, and I don't tell you enough how proud I am to be your grandson. Thank you. For everything."

There is not a dry eye in the courtyard once we are done. We turn back to each other, and kiss. There's no need for vows, or promises. We both believe that it's more important for us to show each other our love. If we've learned anything from all we've gone through, it's that words need to be proven, and love has to be shown. We do that every day.

"Are you ready for your last surprise, Mi Reina Hermosa?"

"Show me what you've got."

We lead everyone down through the streets to the village below. I don't know what I was expecting, but it certainly wasn't Ed Sheeran standing up on the stage in the middle of the street. He smiles at me before launching into *Thinking Out Loud*. Tonight, Matt will kiss me under the light of a thousand real stars, and I know I'm the luckiest woman in the world.

Turn the page for a sneak peek of
***Society Girls: Sierra*, available January 2016!**

THE *BEGINNING*

<u>Sierra</u>

When Reina Corrigan calls and asks you to come to her office, you don't say no. At least, I don't, and I think I'd be hard pressed to find anyone else who'd say no to her, either. She's intimidating as hell, even though I know she's super cool, too. Anyway, here I am, waiting in the lobby of the Corrigan & Co. Foundation. Trying not to bite my nails, or fidget too much as Alex Corrigan smiles at me.

"You can go in now, Sierra," she tells me.

"Thanks."

I make my way down the hall and raise my hand to knock. The double doors of Reina's office open before my hand can connect. I chuckle as I look inside, seeing my sister-in-law, Ainsley, and her friend Darcy inside the office as well as Reina and Jane Corrigan.

"Please come in, Sierra," Reina tells me with a smile.

I walk in and take the open seat next to Darcy. "I didn't realize this was a group thing," I say, pulling at the bottom of my patterned blouse as I bite my lip." I have no idea why I'm here, and I'm honestly even more confused right now than I was sitting out there waiting.

"I'm sorry for all of the secrecy, but even though you know what we really do here, what we need to discuss with you is something new, and well, pretty exciting for us."

I *do* know what really goes on here. Besides the great work the Foundation does publicly, they do even more privately. The women of the Society are spies. Ten agents who go undercover, and help right the wrongs that are committed against those who can't protect themselves. They also sometimes take on private jobs, like figuring out who's trying to sabotage a football team. Which is how I found out about them—they saved me, my brother, and a whole football stadium full of players and fans.

Ainsley was undercover, and while Zack was pissed at her for it, I was intrigued. Since then, she's taught me how to shoot a gun and use other weapons, how to hack into computer systems, and some other really cool things. There's never been a guarantee that a Society position would open up, but I'm in a good position should that happen. I'm hoping it's happening right now.

"What's new?" I ask, trying to hide my excitement.

"As you are well aware, every woman in the Society is currently married, some are having babies, and pretty much everyone has been in the public eye recently. As a result, we've decided to bring in a whole new group of women, all at once for the first time, to train as agents."

"Yes."

"We haven't asked you anything, my dear." Jane reminds me with a smile.

"Oh. I just thought…I mean…why am I here?"

"So we can ask you if you want to try to become one of us," Darcy tells me with a laugh.

"Yes. I want to. Yes." I don't even care that I sound like an idiot. I *want* this.

"It's not going to be easy. You will have to pass ten different areas of training. Some may be easier for you than others, but all need to be mastered. There's only pass or fail with us. We can't have it any other way, because when we go out on missions, lives are at stake," Reina tells me.

"I understand."

"I've shown her some things already. I have faith in her," Ainsley says.

"Thanks," I tell her.

"We all have faith in you, Sierra. You wouldn't be here otherwise," Reina lets me know.

"What do I have to do?"

"For right now, nothing. I—we—want to take the time to make sure we do this right, since it's never been done before with ten women at once. I am anticipating that it will take almost a year to get this all pulled together. During this time, keep the job you just took in Seattle, and go about your daily life almost like you normally would."

"Almost?"

"Yes," she tells me with a smile. "I want you to pay closer attention to what is going on around you. Both in your daily interactions, and in the news. While you may not be officially training yet, it's going to be beneficial for you to start working on things already. Keep going to the gun range, and working on your computer skills."

"Okay. I can do that. There's just one thing." It's something I'm worried about because of what she said about why they are doing this.

"You're worried about being in the spotlight."

"Yes. There have been some new stories on our family, and while I'm not a household name, there are people who know who I am." That just comes with the territory when your brother's a football god.

"We're actually thinking we can use it to our advantage. Just like with Ainsley, Darcy, Audrey, and me, you'll be invited places that we need to get into. Other times, we'll teach you how to disguise yourself to blend in."

"That's a relief."

"You wouldn't be here if Reina thought there'd be a problem," Jane tells me.

"So when the year is up, what happens?"

"It may be less than a year, but when the time comes, you'll move into an apartment in our building, and start training. Darcy will be mentoring you, and while you'll have some free time, most of your days and nights will be spent trying to pass your classes."

"You're mentoring me, Darce?" I ask.

"Yes. When you let me hide out with you last year, you told me you wanted to be one of us, and also that you didn't want it to be because I was kicked out. You impressed me, and I want the chance to help you through this. I won't go easy on you, but I'll support you however I can."

"I didn't think I could be impartial," Ainsley explains, looking worried.

"It's fine," I tell her. "I can't wait to work with all of you, and I'm glad to have Darcy as my mentor. I won't fail. I promise"

I mean it. Failure is not an option for me. I want to be a part of the Society more than I've ever wanted anything else in my life. Yes, I went to college, and I've been working in an auction house for the last couple of years, but I've never felt like that was my calling. This—the Society—is what I've wanted since I knew it existed. No matter what they throw at me, I'll pass these classes. I have to.

* * *

One year later

Sierra

It's finally here. Day one of my training in the Society. Today we're getting all of our security clearances, filling out forms, receiving our class schedules, and moving into our apartments. It feels a little like college again, but more intense. There are four other girls with me in the elevator that's descending to the bowels of the Corrigan & Co. building. I don't recognize any of them, but I smile at them, and they smile back.

Stepping off the elevator, I hear a yell, and then I'm enveloped in a hug. By no less than a princess. "Hi Jen," I tell her with a laugh.

"I'm so glad to see you, Si."

Jenysis is Darcy's husband's cousin. He gave up his kingdom for her, and Jen's dad took over as king, making her a princess. She was a Lady before, I think. All I know is that I'm as glad to see her as she is to see me. We met over a year ago, and we've stayed in contact. Of course, neither of us could tell the other we were being recruited.

"You too."

"I didn't realize I was walking into a sorority house," a bitchy looking blonde says with a sneer on her face.

"So not a sorority girl," I say, glaring right back at her. "Not that it's really any of your business."

"Actually, anything that goes on with one of you will be important to all of you," Reina says, walking in with a scowl on her face, and her girls at her back. "The bond you form with one another is just as important as the training you'll be receiving. You'll have to depend on each other, and trust each other, while you're on missions. And during training, it will be the support and help from your friends that will help you get through this training. I've leaned on these nine women more than I ever thought I would, and they all know I'd do the same for them. Sisterhood is paramount to us. We would never hurt, or betray each other, and we expect you all to feel the same way about each other. Do you understand?"

"Yes."

"Good. Let's get started."

Darcy comes over and gives me a hug before leading me to her office. I take a seat, and she motions to a packet on the table in front of me.

"This has everything you need to know for right now in it. Someone from Ainsley's team will be by to do your hand and retina scans. Those will get you into the elevators and our rooms here, as well as your apartment. Chloe Griffin took your color choices and style into consideration, and created an apartment for you that I think you'll love. Your place isn't as big as ours, but if you pass, you'll be moved to a custom place like ours on a higher floor."

"I'm sure the apartment will be perfect." Hell, I'd live in a box if it meant I could work here.

She nods, and then looks serious. "We have to go over the results of the tests we had you take last month."

"Okay."

"You scored high in technology, weapons, sparring, fashion, and research. You did okay in analysis, etiquette, science, and blending. Languages is where it looks like we may have a problem."

"I took Spanish in high school. I still remember most of it."

"I know. That helps a little, but you're going to need to master at least three other languages, and once of them has to be complex. I think you'll be fine with French, and Italian for two of them. For the other one, you can choose between Arabic, Portuguese, Chinese, Japanese, Hebrew, Turkish, or Russian."

"Do I have to decide now?" I ask, panicking. I knew training wouldn't be easy, but I didn't expect a big obstacle so soon.

"Not right now, but Reina will want to know what you choose by the end of the week so she can plan out your studies."

"Reina is teaching languages?"

"Yes. She's fluent in pretty much every language on the planet."

"Wow."

Society Weddings ⋆ 167

"Yeah, I know. She's all that, and a bag of chips. No pressure for the rest of us."

"What are you teaching?"

"You can't laugh."

"Okay," I tell her with a shrug. I know she used to be a cat burglar, so I'm guessing it's blending.

"Etiquette."

"Oh."

"Yeah, oh. Apparently all of my princess training has made me the expert. It's pretty embarrassing."

"I think you're still a bad-ass."

"Thanks."

We spend the rest of the day going over the paperwork I need to fill out, my salary while training—which is more than in a month than I made in the last year an assistant at the auction house in Seattle—and various policies and procedures. Basically, everyone else in the building will think we are Foundation interns, and we have to act the part. It's a simple form of on the job training, but an important one. We can't slip up. Not that I intend to. I had no problem playing the part of intern while flirting with the junior execs from C&C in the cafeteria this morning. Now I just need to worry about mastering a complex language.

ACKNOWLEDGEMENTS

From the bottom of my heart, I want to thank everyone who's supported me since I started writing. My friends who believed in me from the first page of Gaming For Love, the team who helps me get my books ready for you, and all of you who sent me a kind word, or left me a good review after reading my books. You're all important to me, and I wouldn't still be writing without you! Lots of virtual hugs and love from me to you!

ABOUT THE AUTHOR

Crystal Perkins has always been a big reader, but she never thought she would write her own book, until she did. She lives in Las Vegas, where you can find her running author events and selling books at conventions when she isn't reading, buying too many Sherlock t-shirts online or finding a place to put all of her Pop! figurines. A mac and cheese connoisseur, she travels the country looking for the perfect version, while attending book conventions and signings as a cover for her research. The Griffin Brothers series and the Corrigan & Co. series are international best sellers, and she's thankful to the readers who made those things happen!

Find her here:
www.crystalperkinsauthor.com
facebook.com/crystalperkinsauthor
@wondermomlv
crystal@crystalperkinsauthor.com

Printed in Great Britain
by Amazon